A Study in Bourbon:
Odd Fictions & Other Lies

J.E. Tobal

Copyright © 2014, 2019 J.E. Tobal

First Revised Edition

Kjaha'sy Press

Cover Design by J.E. Tobal

All rights reserved.

The following is a work of fiction. The characters, circumstances, and dialogue are products of the author's imagination. Any resemblance to persons living or dead is entirely coincidental.

ISBN: 1501076221
ISBN-13: 9781501076220

FOR

Harsh Spaceghost Kumar

CONTENTS

Odd Fictions & Other Lies

1	Apocrypha	4
2	Fuck You, Stephenie Meyer	53
3	Fuck You, J.E. Tobal	74

A Single Sentence

4	Buddha the Destroyer	93
5	The Three Weddings of Galilee	122
6	The Tenth Crusade	144

PREFACE

This is probably where a normal author would write something inspirational about the stories they've written. Something about the journey of writing and all that nonsense. They'd thank those that helped them along the way and would probably make some sort of cute comment about their pet dog, Geraldo, and the intricate role he plays in the author's family life.

However, I'm an idiot.

In place of that relatively egocentric author's rant, I thought I'd just briefly impart some random information about each of the stories contained in this volume. Some of the information will be insightful. Some of the information will be questionable, at best. Some of the information will probably (maybe) be a lie.

Though one thing you should know is that I drink a lot of alcohol. Often to excess. Especially when I write. And in these bourbon-fueled sessions, I often continue to write well past the point where I have blacked out and no longer remember anything I've written. I wake up in the morning, look at my computer screen, and pray to God that I haven't written the phrase, "I like boobies" over and over.

Considering how often I feel the bourbon is more in charge than I am when I write, you'd almost think that's where I got the idea to call this collection, 'A Study in Bourbon'.

Almost.

Apocrypha – 2013

This was the first story I wrote after finishing my novel, *A Kind of Drug*. Not surprisingly, I wanted to write something that was radically different in nearly every way from that story. So there's spaceships and alien creatures and philosophy on physics and nearly no vulgarity at all and then everyone in the world dies….

Okay, so it's not RADICALLY different from *A Kind of Drug*. Shut up.

Fuck You, Stephenie Meyer – 2010

The thing I love about this story is how seriously it's taken online by total strangers. If you haven't before, PLEASE take a moment to read the comments left by Twilight fans on Amazon.com. There's a lot of people out there who want me dead.

And in case you don't know, Stephenie Meyer is the author of Twilight. And this story is about vampires who need semen to live instead of blood.

I'm not nearly as funny as I think I am.

Fuck You, J.E. Tobal - 2015

I really just thought if I could tell Stephenie Meyer to go fuck herself, then I could certainly tell myself to go fuck myself, too.

Buddha the Destroyer – 2011

I struggled with the ending of this story a lot. At one point there was even a talking parrot involved. Seriously.

The Three Weddings of Galilee – 2008

This was the start of the 'A Single Sentence' series. I got the idea from a line in The Wife of Bath's tale in Chaucer's Canterbury Tales (because I'm a pretentious, English Major, shit wagon). Basically, she posits how unfair it is that a woman can only marry one man all due to the fact that Jesus himself only attended a single wedding (in Galilee). Well, I thought, what if he attended three? So, I wrote a story about that. And only killed one character off in the process. That's practically a happy ending for me.

The other two stories in the series (and the subsequent others that will come in time) are all about the same subject matter: What would the world be like if just one, single sentence was different in a critical, historical work.

Hence the title. As if you hadn't figured that out yet.

The Tenth Crusade – 2013

My ability to take a revolutionary story about massive upheaval and societal change and add in a number of dick jokes and references to blow jobs is really accentuated here. So, pat on the back for me.

APOCRYPHA

I.

It was late November when the spacecraft landed. The expansive plains of western Utah were cool and windy as it glided down from the heavens like it had every right to be there. Nothing detected it, however. No radars. No satellites. No infrared sensors. Mostly because the spacecraft had chosen not to be detected. Some people thought that was absurd. How could it choose not to be detected? But when The Machine was posed with that question, it didn't understand where the confusion lay. And so, it responded in kind.

"That's a sort of silly question, isn't it? Haven't you ever chosen to not be noticed when you enter a room, maybe late at night? You remove your shoes and tip toe across the floor? Maybe crawl on hands and knees? Or turn off the lights and sneak through in the darkness? Why would you even ask that? Of course it can choose to not be detected. Why wouldn't it be able to do that?"

Or, at least, that's how it sounded to Lou.

The spacecraft continued its descent onto the desert. Impossibly huge. Ten miles wide. Half a mile high. Small probes, no bigger than footballs, circled around it. They flew out and returned. Orbited and escaped. They seemed to be made of stone and iron. Ivory and glass. Wood and water. Everything and nothing all at once. Just like the spacecraft. The probes were just miniature versions of their father. And they served him well. They knew of nothing else.

    The spacecraft didn't make any noise as it touched the ground. It didn't shake the earth. It didn't rattle the sky. It casually touched the ground like a princess stepping out of a pumpkin carriage. Gracefully. Delicately. Not with thunder or malice. Not with violent power. But with all the grandeur and magnificence of a deity that does not need to express its presence to the ground. The ground knows better. It gives way. Is subservient. Just as it should be.

    Once the spacecraft had landed, it spent a day gathering nearby atmospheric data. It surveyed the land for pockets and reserves of precious metals. It studied the waters and their mineral contents. Then, one day, a relatively small door opened on one side. It wasn't an impressive door. It was neither ornate nor even marked as an opening. But it opened, nonetheless. And for the first time ever, The Machine set itself down onto Earth's dry land.

    It moved forward, away from the spacecraft. Its intent was not to go very far. Within the spacecraft, it had detected a nearby plateau and it wished to reach the summit. From there, The Machine would take a personal survey to determine how it would begin its operation.

    Of course, The Machine never made it to the plateau. Only a handful of meters outside of the spacecraft, it ran into the silliest of characters. Two of them, in fact. There, just outside the door where The Machine had emerged from, were two cowboys. Not some sort of picturesque, beautiful, Hollywood cowboys, but rustic men. Poorly educated and aggressive with yellow teeth and rotten livers. They were covered in cotton and sweat. Leather and dirt. Confusion and firearms. They had found the spacecraft by complete accident. A few of their cattle had gone astray into the same valley the spacecraft had landed in. The cowboys had then followed the cattle with the intent of wrangling the cows back into the herd. But before the men could catch their stray animals, they came across a strange structure that didn't belong in the landscape.

The two men sat atop their horses and stared at the spacecraft, confused, while their livestock galloped off into the nearby hills. They were dumbfounded. Stupefied. Forget never seeing anything like this in their lives, they had never even imagined anything like this. An entire valley filled by a single, foreign arrangement of impossibilities. Spires rising up from the surface of the craft like unicorn horns. Threads floating off of it, shimmering and beautiful like angel hair. The two men argued whether or not the color of the craft was pitch black or pale white.

Both were right. Both were wrong.

While the cowboys watched the craft and debated, they were completely unaware of The Machine's approach. It casually moved toward them and didn't stop until it was only a few feet away from their horse's scared eyes. The Machine had not expected them or their horses. Had not expected this. Had not expected life. For the first time in a hundred thousand years, The Machine was unsure of how to proceed.

When the cowboys noticed The Machine, they were not happy. They were not sad. They were not angry. The best way to describe their emotional state was, "scared beyond rational thought". They didn't understand The Machine. They saw rock and mirror. Bone and copper. Steel and mercury. And they were confused. They responded to this confusion and fear the same way they had been trained to respond to it since they were children. Both men drew their guns.

The Machine, naturally, didn't understand the gesture. Nor did it understand concepts like fear or prejudice. But it did know that it needed to stretch its arms in order to fully understand the scene. And so, it did. The Machine slowly began to outstretch its ten thousand, impossible arms.

The cowboys did not like this.

Aiming for what he could only assume was its head, one of the men shot at The Machine. Unfortunately, the bullet ricocheted and struck the other man directly in the face. He fell over, clutching his left eye and screaming in agony. It only took a minute or so for the loss of blood to render the poor man unconscious and, eventually, dead. Both the other cowboy and The Machine watched as the injured man clung to life and then, hopelessly, lost his grip.

The Machine did not fully understand life, but it did understand death. And so, it then acknowledged the remaining cowboy by speaking its first words after landing onto this, our planet Earth.

"So," The Machine said. "This is awkward."

II.

"So, are you two dating or something?"

"Hm?" Lou asked as he looked up from his cell phone. He had already forgotten the name of the guy talking to him. They had only been introduced a few hours ago, but Lou did that a lot. Forget people's names, that is. He never forgot a face. But names? He never cared for them. There were people that Lou had met six or seven times and still didn't know their names. And this character was no exception.

"You and Eden. Are you boyfriend and girlfriend? Or just early on in your relationship? What's your story?"

Lou let out a quick chuckle and looked back down toward his phone. He had several missed calls, all from a blocked number. He was perplexed. He spoke without looking up from his phone. "We're exes, actually."

"Wait, really?" the mystery guy asked, surprised. "But you two have such great chemistry together."

"Yeah, tell me about it." Lou was only half-paying

attention to the mystery guy. He was texting a couple of his friends to see if they had any information as to his unknown, yet repeated caller.

"Well, are you two okay with that?"

"Not really. Well, I guess she is. Though I've been trying to convince her of how much of a moron she is for years now."

"Really? Why'd you break up then, if you don't mind me asking?"

"Didn't I just explain that? It's 'cause she's a complete moron," Lou said, right as Eden was walking back over to join the conversation. He said it without looking up from his phone even though he saw Eden approach out of the corner of his eye. "I mean, she's gotta be one of the dumbest girls I've ever…" He trailed off intentionally as he looked up at Eden.

"So," Lou began. "This is awkward."

Lou smiled at Eden. Eden smiled back. Her smile wrapped itself around his heart.

The ballad of Lou and Eden began three years ago when a mutual friend introduced the two of them. When he first met Eden, Lou thought she was attractive and fun, but never thought anything would ever come of his mild infatuation. At the time, he was heavily invested in his master's degree at Columbia University and was already loosely dating another girl he had met three months prior. But still, Eden captivated him. Lou loved how she was full of ideas and spontaneity. Adventure and wonderment. Fire and brimstone.

And oh, how Lou loved fire and brimstone.

Eden gave Lou her phone number that night and it was only a matter of days before the two were inseparable. Friends who had known Lou for years were asking him where this girl had been all his life. The man who ran the local laundromat smiled and patted them on the back every Saturday when they came in to wash their laundry together. A mere six months after they met, Eden's mother asked her daughter how much longer he'd wait before proposing to her.

Eden and Lou were yin and yang. Morning moon and evening sun. Magic and machinery.

This was because of who they were. Lou was practical and logical. Sound and reasonable. Eden, on the other hand, was quixotic and uncontrollable. Sassy and unpredictable.

The two broke each other. Eden found herself getting upset at Lou if he was more than 10 minutes late for a mere phone call. Lou, in contrast, loved how Eden would wake up in the morning and suggest they travel fifty miles out into the country just to eat pancakes and eggs.

But they were young and they were stupid. And like all young and stupid people, they made young and stupid mistakes. Lou's was of arrogance. Eden's was of fear.

Lou, midway through his long, hard road into a PhD in mechanical engineering, suddenly began questioning his relationship with a waitress. With a girl who had barely finished high school. Who preferred to watch movies than read a book. Who knew more about wine than about water.

Eden, on the other hand, was realizing that Lou was everything she had ever wanted in a husband. He was thoughtful, intelligent, hilarious, attractive, and would rip the eyes out anyone who looked at her the wrong way. But Eden was still young. Even though she knew she wanted to get married one day, she wasn't ready for that day just yet. She still couldn't help but to see that day coming in Lou. And she was petrified.

And so, without knowing what else to do with their love and their confusion, Lou and Eden made the firm decision to ruin their relationship. Less than a year before their beautiful affair had begun, it was already over.

Three months later, Lou was having a beer with his best friend. "What in the hell have I done?" he asked his friend. "It wasn't Eden's job that I was in love with. Her lack of math skills didn't make her any less beautiful. She was an angel with a perfect heart. A perfect soul. And I was too much of a blind asshole to see it. She's gone forever now. I'll never be in her grace again."

You see, with a wild girl comes wild emotions. Even though Lou had realized what he'd done wrong, it was already too late. Eden wouldn't have him back. He pleaded with her. He begged her to try it one more time. He wept and cried and promised her eternity.

But Eden had already placed a clean and beautiful layer of ice over her heart. Hurt by someone once, she made sure they would never be able to hurt her again. She numbed herself to them. This also made it easier for her to begin dating a coworker – a man she didn't even like very much – merely seven weeks after her relationship with Lou burned away to ash. He helped her to forget Lou's smile. To forget the way Lou laughed at all of her jokes, no matter how awful they were. To forget how Low could make her feel like she could be anything she wanted to be, no matter how unreasonable the dream. Eden had convinced herself that Lou was nothing but a fling. A fleeting affair. One in a series of dead-end relationships.

But despite what her mind told her, Eden's heart knew better. And every time one of her true, dead-end relationships ran briskly off a cliff, she called Lou. They would talk for hours and laugh and cry and be so happy to be back in each other's lives. Not as lovers, but as friends. Months would pass where the two would rekindle a strange form of friendship and Lou would regain a certain kind of sparkle in his eyes. But soon, Eden would find herself back in the arms of another man and Lou would crumble. Lou couldn't stand to see Eden with another man and he'd soon break contact with her. But then one day his phone would ring and he'd hear Eden's sweet voice and his resolve would waste away.

This happened over and over, time and time again, for two years. Eventually, one day, Eden was single again and Lou spoke to her without restraint.

"I love you," he said one night over drinks. "And not as a friend. Don't mix my words. I want to spend the rest of my life with you. I know you don't feel the same way as I do and that's fine. I mean, I hate it, but it's fine. I just don't want you to think that when we see each other, I only want to be friends. You know I'll never touch you or hurt you or anything like that, but still. I love you more than I can even imagine. Are you okay with that?"

"Oh, sweet potato," Eden said. "I can't even imagine my life without you anymore. Just please don't leave me again. You've done it too many times and it hurts too much. You're too important in my life. Promise me?"

Lou promised with every ounce of his heart but could never figure out if it was the worst or best promise he ever made in his life.

On rare occasions, the two would go out and drink themselves to excess at a bar or a friend's house. These were the best days of Lou's life. Primarily because Eden would be too intoxicated to go home by herself and so she'd find herself staying at Lou's place for the night. She's slip herself into some of Lou's old clothes and, as if he were in a dream, he'd fall asleep next to the woman loved.

"You're just killing yourself," Lou's friends told him. "Why do you let her do this to you? Send her home, already."

"I know," he'd reply. "But she's absolute paradise to me. And a taste of paradise is better than no paradise at all, right? You don't understand what it is to me to wake up with Eden next to me."

Lou's friends just shook their heads and gave up. What was there to say to a man in love?

And it was around this time when Lou found himself talking to a man at a holiday party who was inquiring about Lou and Eden's relationship. Lou placed his phone back in his pocket and ignored the texts and calls he continued to receive for the rest of the evening.

After all, nothing in his life was more important than Eden.

And so, as the holiday party wound to a close, Eden once again found herself sleeping at Lou's home for the night. Just before she fell asleep, Lou spoke to her. "I'm still waiting for you to come to your senses and marry me, you know."

"I know," she said. "Me, too."

III.

When Eden awoke, late the next morning, Lou was missing from his bed. She naturally assumed he was in the bathroom or getting something to drink and so she just rolled over and continued to lightly doze. But after another thirty minutes passed without Lou returning, she became concerned. Eden rubbed her eyes, sat up, and left the bedroom.

She found Lou sitting on the couch in his living room. He was talking on his cell phone with one hand and furiously writing down a number of details with the other. She noticed sweat all around his face and neck. His skin seemed pale and he was breathing in short, shallow gasps. And even though he wasn't saying much, the few words he spoke sounded abrupt and tense.

Lou acknowledged Eden when she walked into the room, but then he immediately went back to his phone and his notes. Eden, not knowing what else to do, sat down in a nearby chair and simply stared at him. She had never seen him this stressed. Her mind was going to a million horrible places.

She imagined that his mother had died; a poor woman, twice divorced, who lived further away than she cared to be from her three children. She imagined that his doctorate work was being trivialized and rejected and that he wouldn't be able to receive his long sought after PhD. She even imagined that some secret and mysterious lover of his was phoning him with details of a surprise arrival and he was nervous knowing that Eden was only in the next room.

Naturally, the cause of Lou's tension was none of these things.

"You okay, Lucy," she asked him as he finally hung up the phone. It was one of her old nicknames for him; a name she had only seldom used in the years since they had ended their romantic relationship.

Lou took several deep breaths. His right leg was rapidly and uncontrollably bouncing up and down. His face was a mash of apprehension and surprise. Tension and fear. Confusion and misery.

"I have to go to Utah," he said finally.

"What?" Eden asked, shocked. "Why?"

"I'm not entirely sure, really. I just got the longest lecture about national security and how I should be answering my phone in a more-timely manner. Apparently when they couldn't get a hold of me, they contacted my mother and scared the life out of her. She started calling me at seven in the morning telling me to answer my mystery call."

"Oh my God! What's going on? Is everything okay? And who's 'they'?"

"Yeah, still not sure about any of that. Especially the 'they' part. All I know is that I'm leaving for Utah. Today. A ticket's already been booked for me. I have to pack for, and I quote, an indefinite period of time. All I know is that I'm going on this trip at the request of Dr. Harris and that I have a very strange series of books I'm supposed to brush up on during my flight."

"So, it's about your degree?" Eden asked, still not entirely sure as to what Lou was saying.

"No, I don't think so. This seems..." Lou trailed off as he looked at the short list of books again. "I don't know. Something weird is definitely going on. These books. They're...they don't have practical applications. I don't understand what the emergency could be in regards to nanocarbon fibers and their behavior in ultra-high gravity environments."

"Okay," Eden said, unsure of how to react. "Well,

do you want me to leave? If you've got a lot to sort out, I don't want to be in your way."

"Angel, if there's ever been a time in my life when I want you here, it's right now."

With that, Eden stood up and sat herself next to Lou on the couch. She then used her right arm to give him a sort of combination back rub, massage, and caress. All the while, Lou just held his head in his hands as he felt that, if he didn't, his brain would surely explode from out his skull. Eventually, slowly, the color began to return to his face.

"Want me to help you pack then?" Eden asked, giving Lou one final rub against his neck.

"Please," he said. "I feel like if I don't get some help, I'm gonna forget to pack things like pants right now."

"Hey! Sounds like my sort of party!" she said and Lou gave a short laugh. "Okay, come on. You start to pack and I'll make you some breakfast. If you play your cards right, I'll even take you to the airport. You're lucky I've got a thing for smart guys."

"Awwwww," Lou said as Eden stood up and walked back into his bedroom. "Come on, now you're just being mean."

IV.

Once on board the plane, Lou finally discovered why he had been called into the western desert. Sort of. His supervising professor – an extremely elderly man named Dr. Richard Harris – was the actual person called into the endeavor. Dr. Harris, however, was pushing ninety years old and wanted someone else there with him. He knew that his mind was not as agile as it used to be (nor was his body, for that matter) and that he should have a younger, more creative counterpart at his side. Therefore, he insisted that Lou Absalom, the most brilliant of his students, join him in

A STUDY IN BOURBON

this odd and secretive mission.

Of course, as he boarded the plane, he still only received strange, blank stares from all the government suits whenever he asked about what it was he was actually needed for.

Upon arriving in Utah, things got stranger. He imagined he'd be going to some research facility in Salt Lake City. Or maybe some secret government base in the desert. Now, Lou did land out in desert, but it was at some tiny airfield that looked like it hadn't been used since long before Lou had even been born. He was immediately escorted to a 'secured facility' by means of a helicoptered military detail. In reality, this 'secured facility' was a just an old ranch house that had been commandeered and militarized by the US government. Lou thought it looked about as hospitable as a barbed-wire enema. He took one look at his shoddy accommodations and then back at his military escorts. "Well, you boys sure know how to show a girl a good time," he said sarcastically.

Of course, Lou soon found out that he wasn't the only scientist staying in the unsecure secured facility. Sharing these accommodations with him were about two dozen other very uniquely qualified field specialists. Yes, Lou always knew that he knew more about mechatronics and biomechatronics than any other ten people on earth, but so what? Every engineer and scientist had some sort of specialty field. That wasn't anything new.

But what was new was Lou being called into the middle of the desert to share a bunk bed with a molecular biologist. And a multi-linguist. And an astrobiologist. And an astrophysicist. And two psychologists.

Of course, the even weirder part about all of it was that Lou was still working on his PhD while all his other "bunkmates" were men and women all well into their prime. These were people in their forties and fifties. They had all made a name for themselves years ago as pioneers of their degrees. Lou felt like a little kid among such giants and wasn't sure if Dr. Harris had made the right call with bringing him along for this strange ride. He went to bed that night angry and confused. Scared and lonely. Shaken and lost.

The next morning, Lou was awoken and herded outside along with his new roommates. He was put on a bus with fifty-two other scientists and driven to a massive camouflaged tent that had been erected during the night. There, all of the confused scientists were finally told why they were in the desert. They were going to be the first people on earth to ever have a conversation with a being from another world.

Or, not really a being, as it were. But a Machine.

"We haven't formed a line of communication with it yet," the General said. Lou knew that the General had announced his name earlier, but as usual, he had already forgotten what it was. The same went for the other scientists, too. He made a note of some of their professions, but that was it. Lou couldn't remember the name of his sister's boyfriend. How was ever expected to remember the names of fifty-some-odd strangers?

"After first contact," the General continued, "The Machine sequestered itself back into its ship and hasn't come out since. We've setup a number of defensive measures since it has already killed a civilian, even if it was an accident. We did not, however, want to try to approch and open a dialogue with this entity without the lot of you; our very planned and thought out team of specialists. We are hoping that, with all of your help, we can communicate with this entity peacefully and civilly."

And so, around 3pm on a seemingly normal Thursday in November, fifty-three scientists and a rather sizeable military detail gathered and approached the spacecraft. As they neared it, the spacecraft opened its doors with an easy casualness. Then, The Machine came out to greet them.

Everyone froze as The Machine approached them. It was like nothing they could've ever expected. With every movement, it seemed to change and alter its appearance.

A STUDY IN BOURBON

Appendages that appeared to be legs for one moment soon bent and flickered and turned into tails the next. A carapace that looked to be some sort of partial exoskeleton rotated and twisted until shone like polished mirror. Pistons hammered and stretched until the movements became so fluid that the machinery looked as though it simply turned into liquid.

Now, the government had long, long ago created a prioritized list of questions to be asked if humans were to ever encounter an extraterrestrial. These questions had been explained to the team of scientists and the General knew them by heart. But upon seeing such a strange and bizarre creation, every one of their minds buckled and turned into sludge. Rather than asking if The Machine came in peace, the awestruck General just asked the first and only question on his mind.

"Dear God in Heaven, where do you come from?" the General asked.

"A military bunker deep inside a mountain on another planet," heard the General.

"Everywhere and nowhere," heard one of the linguists.

"I don't know, but my first true memories are of the spacecraft," heard a psychologist.

Lou and his professor, on the other hand, heard a detailed description of an advanced, mechanical factory.

Everyone began to murmur. To spread rumors and tales. They spoke of their own, personal interpretation of The Machine's answer.

The linguists, however, were quite confused. They asked The Machine to speak again.

"What would you like me to say?" The Machine asked. Everyone began to mumble again. It was hundreds of whispered demands and questions, but no outright requests.

"You seem to know our language," a philosopher said. "Do you know what poetry is?"

"I do," The Machine replied.

"Tell us the saddest poem you know then."

The Machine spoke. Everyone listened. And everyone cried.

"It's speaking in tongues," one linguist began to explain, as she wiped the saltwater from her eyes.

"How do you mean?" one of the biologists asked.

"I'm going to ask it to tell a different poem, equally as sad. I ask you all to remember nothing but the first two lines you hear. All of you. Okay?" She said this as she pulled a small tape recorder out of her pocket.

The scientists all nodded their heads in consent. The Machine told a second poem that was just as beautiful and horrible as the last. It seemed impossible. How could a robot from another planet know such beautiful pieces of work that could affect everyone so profoundly?

"Okay, now, you," the linguist said, still wiping her second set of tears from her eyes. She was pointing at Lou. "What were the first two lines of the poem?"

"I once met a desert," Lou began. "That dreamt of the rain."

"Very good," the linguist said. "And you?" she asked, looking toward the biochemist.

"Is this a trick?" he asked. "Cause that's not what it said at all."

"No, good. That's the point," the linguist said. "Please, give us your interpretation."

One of the psychologists looked at The Machine. "And this…this thing is okay with us just sitting here bantering?"

"If it's not," the General began. "Then we have much deeper problems in front of us."

"Ah," the psychologist said. "Well, ummm…this is what I heard: Three drops of rain once fell in a rainforest, They were the last that ever touched the ground."

"Someone's an environmentalist, aren't they?" the linguist asked.

"Maybe? What difference does that make?"

"None, really. But I had a theory. You've all just

proved it. Here, listen," the linguist said and rewound the tape recorder. "Listen, this is what we just heard."

The linguist played back the audio and everyone once again heard the beautiful poem. Once again, eyes watered and knees buckled. Then she stopped the recording, flicked a couple of switches, and played the audio again. This time, the audio was played backward, instead of forward.

From the recorder came a strange burst of screams and wails and whispers. Birds calls and whales songs. Digital noises and mechanical creaks. Organic mischief and automatic disorder.

"It's gibberish," the linguist said again. "Perfect gibberish. It's saying everything and nothing at all. I know some of my colleagues were curious as to whether or not this Machine was going to be a Chinese Room. Well, forget it. This magnificent construct is not a Chinese Room. In fact, compared to it, we are the Chinese Room. Ask it anything, it will reply. I'll drop dead on this spot if there's a question we can ask it to which it cannot reply. It's a repository of knowledge and, for all intents and purposes, knows everything. We're simply translating to the best of our brain's ability whatever it wants to tell us. So, if we hear different descriptions or different poems or things in different languages, it's simply because we're understanding a purer version of what it's trying to tell us. Anything we can't understand? Well, that's 'cause we lack the understanding as an individual. Which is why we all understood it to come from different places and we all heard different poems."

That's about when order gave way to chaos. Every one of the fifty-three scientists asked a question to The Machine and demanded they be answered first. It was a cacophony of scientific demands. The Machine began to reply, simply at random.

"What is your name or designation?" one man asked.

"I have none," The Machine replied. "I am the only

one of my kind. No name or designation was required. I simply am."

"Your age then," an woman asked. "When were you constructed?"

"Never," was the reply. "And always. I am without birth. I have existed always and will continue to exist always. I cannot be killed. I cannot be created."

A number of people did not like this reply. Specifically, the General. He did not like hearing about some alien construct that was infinite and could not be killed. It was he that was answered next.

"Why are you on our planet, then? Speak your purpose."

"Mining," The Machine said. Many people murmured. It seemed like such a simple answer for such a complex situation.

"Is that all you want?" one of the biologists asked. "Minerals?"

"Yes," The Machine said.

"Then why have you not begun your mining operation?"

"Because you're alive," The Machine said. This answer shushed most of the crowd. All except one. All except Lou.

"Why is that a problem? And why have you come to our planet now? If you're eternal, why have you only just now made it to our planet? Where were you before you came here?"

The Machine roared and growled. Whispered and sang. This was a question it found interesting.

"My creation myth," heard Lou. "This is what you wish to hear, yes?"

"Yes," he affirmed, uncertainly. And then he added, "Why here? Why now?"

"Once upon a time," The Machine began. "There was a great civilization. Alien and far away, it became so advanced that it's need for resources far surpassed that of quarries and oil rigs. After their population exceeded one hundred and fifty billion lifeforms, they soon realized that their single solar system could not sustain their needs. This is when I was constructed."

"So, you were built at some point?" the General interrupted.

"Yes," The Machine replied. "However, that was before time began. Before I existed, there was no time."

"I don't understa…" the General said.

"Shut up," the microbiologist screamed. "Why not try letting the artificially intelligent alien machine speak? That so much to ask?"

The General glared at the microbiologist, but he did stop speaking. The Machine continued.

"I was constructed to sustain them. They required vast quantities of natural resources for their survival, and so I was built to find these resources. To mine them and to send them back to my creators in so that they could survive and could continue to grow and expand."

"How vast?" a mechanical engineer asked. "What sort of natural resources were needed?"

"They required approximately 4.6×10^{16} grams in raw materials each year to sustain their expanding civilization. This mass consists of everything from iron to wood to copper to water to diamonds to unrefined rocks. It is a rough summation of what they require for survival."

"Holy crap," said the geologist. He was the only one of his kind invited to this strange summit. "That's almost the weight of this entire planet. Are you saying it was your intention to strip this planet clean of resources and send them all back to your civilization of origin?"

"That is my purpose, yes."

"And how long have you been at this task?" the geologist asked.

"Since time began."

"What happens when you run into planets such as ours? Ones with life on it, as you already mentioned. You said this was a problem before. Why?" the General asked, cold and scared.

"This is the first planet I've encountered with intelligent life on it since…" after that, the translation got fuzzy. The scientists spoke, but none of them could get a solid consensus on the amount of time it had been since The Machine had met intelligent life.

"Why?" an astrobiologist asked. "Why has it been some strange, unimaginable amount of time since you've met intelligent life? Are we that rare in the galaxy?"

There was a long pause before The Machine spoke again. Everyone held their breath in anticipation of The Machine's reply.

"So," The Machine said eventually. "This is awkward."

"Why?" Dr. Harris asked, unafraid.

"Intelligent life is quite common in this galaxy," The Machine began. "Too common, actually. However, my creators were benevolent. They did not wish me to destroy whole civilizations in order that they reap the benefits. Therefore, I was programmed so that I could not destroy, negatively affect or harm any form of intelligent life. I was only able to mine the planets which contained no form of intelligent life or any form of emerging intelligent life."

"Okay," Lou said. "Sounds great to me."

"The problem was that there were too many planets with intelligence or emerging intelligence on them. It became…troublesome for me."

"Whoa, wait," the astrobiologist said. "Are you saying that intelligent life in the Milky Way was a problem for you?"

"Yes," The Machine said. "I do not care for life. Life is burdensome for me. I seek resources. Life gets in the way."

"And you found a way to end life without ending it yourself, didn't you? You found a loophole," Dr. Harris asked, happy that he wasn't as slow-witted as he imagined himself to be.

"Yes. Quite easily. Your DNA can be manipulated without much effort. This same DNA – or similar enough versions - make up the biological blueprints for nearly all the intelligent creatures throughout the galaxy. And, if reengineered properly, this biological DNA will create a self-destructive species; a lifeform that, eventually, will seek to purposefully destroy itself."

"You mean you've been reengineering all the life in the galaxy to commit suicide? For how long?" the astrobiologist asked.

"Since time began."

"Well, that answers the Fermi Paradox," one astrobiologist replied.

"What's the Fermi Paradox?" the General asked.

"It's a mathematical question of why we haven't found any intelligent life in our galaxy. It seemed to be a logical impossibility. Of course, that got cleared up, oh, ten seconds ago. We haven't met any other intelligent life in our galaxy because this machine has been killing it."

"To be fair," The Machine began. "I killed nothing. I cannot end life. I simply reengineered life to end itself."

"And you've done the same with us, haven't you?" Lou asked, putting the pieces together before anyone else had. "That's why meeting us is so…awkward. We should be long dead, shouldn't we? We should've turned this planet to glass by now. That's why you're here. To mine whatever's left of the planet after we're gone."

"Yes," The Machine said. "I'm still trying to calculate the anomaly. But the transmission should've caused you to destroy yourselves and your planet centuries ago."

This caused an uproar among everyone from the most senior scientist to the lowliest private. A cacophony of outrage that continued until one of the scientists screamed out with a question that silenced the masses.

"Wait, what transmission?" the astronomer asked.

"Radio waves," The Machine replied. "Most biological structures are actually easily manipulated by simple light waves. And once they corrupt a genetic structure, that species will inherently destroy itself, its planet and any planet within ten thousand light years of its location by similar means."

"Wait, what?" one of the psychologists asked. "We haven't destroyed any other civilizations. Hell, we can barely get off our own planet."

"No, but we've created other radio waves, haven't we?" Lou asked.

"Oh, fuck," one of the astrophysicists chimed in. "It's a Von Neumann Probe, isn't it?

"A Von Neumann Probe?" Lou asked.

"It's a self-replicating system," the astrophysicist said. "You create a probe to go out into deep space. That probe lands on another planet and then, using the resources it finds, creates ten other probes. Those ten probes go out and create ten more. And so on.

"That's what these radio waves are. This Machine created the first of them. And when these radio waves hit our planet, they corrupted our DNA. And as we evolved, we inherently created our own radio waves. Nothing more than The Beatles being broadcast on an open frequency. But somehow, some way, the waves are damaged. And one day, these radio waves that we created will reach another planet. They'll reach some species and that species will eventually…turn into us. Turn into a species that will inherently want to destroy its own planet, whether it knows it or not. But before it does, it will create more radio waves. And those waves will affect other planets. And so on.

"That's the Von Neumann probe. These radio waves that this Machine began. They destroy entire planets. And they've been at work since before Earth had its first oceans."

"This thing is our destroyer then," The General said.

"No," one of the psychologists said. "It's our creator."

"Funny," The Machine said. "I detected a difference in your language, however I did not detect a difference in your definitions. I interpreted these two terms to have similar classifications."

"Who is 'they'?" one astrobiologist asked. "What does the civilization that created you call themselves?"

"Untranslatable," The Machine answered.

"What the heck does that mean?" one of the biologists replied, rather angrily. "How can a civilization's name not be translatable into any of our languages?"

"I didn't say they were untranslatable. I said they were untranslatable."

"Does anyone else want to punch this thing?" the same biologist asked.

"Calm down," one of the linguists said. "Remember, he's not saying the name of the civilization is untranslatable. The problem is that what it's trying to tell us is so advanced, so foreign, that we can't even comprehend it. Hell, this civilization could speak in dolphin squeaks for all we know. How would that translate into English? You're just hearing it say, 'Sorry, stupid. You can't understand what I'm trying to tell you.'"

"I don't like that very much," the General said and turned his attention toward The Machine. "What is you and your ship's source of energy?"

The Machine answered.

Four dozen people murmured as they discussed the different answers that The Machine gave them. They discussed black holes and antimatter. Zero-point containment and fourth-dimensions. Electric batteries and old telephones. Of course, the most hilarious answer was the one heard by one of the psychologists.

"Did this thing just say it's powered by magic and wires?" she asked.

"No," Lou said. "They're both powered by a black hole. Somehow – God only knows how – but they've managed to capture one and use it as a power source. This...this machine isn't three dimensional. In order to use the energy of a black hole, it has to be fourth dimensional. At the very least. Which is just about as close to magic and sorcery as you can get, if you don't understand it." Lou thought for a moment and then he looked toward the General. "What was it you said that scared the cowboys?"

"Um," the General stumbled. "Er, something about arms. There were too many of them. They came from nowhere. Something like that. At least, that was the scared confession that I heard from the hungover idiot that met this thing three days ago."

Lou looked at The Machine. "Can you show us your arms?" he asked. "All of them."

"As you wish," The Machine said and, once again, outstretched it's ten thousand arms. They spread like serpents across the landscape. Across the sky. Across the ground. Across everything.

No one could figure out what they were made of. Water and titanium. Bone and carbon. Feathers and ice.

Even though they seemed to come out of The Machine's torso, it was impossible. How could thousands of limbs come out of something only a few feet wide?

"See?" Lou said as The Machine's arms continued to stretch. "Four dimensions."

"Explain this to me now, son," the General said. He watched as The Machine's limbs stretched and grew until they began to block out the sun. As the ground grew dark, the General placed his left hand on the firearm at his hip. "Please, explain it to me now before something bad happens."

"Imagine you're a goldfish in a fish tank," Lou said. "You spend your life happily swimming around and living your life. One day, someone places their fingertip in the surface of the tank. They move it around. You swim up to investigate. You see a small, fleshy object only half the size of your own body. Then, scared, you bite it. As your teeth rip the skin, the fingertip begins to bleed. At first, a little bit of blood. Then more. Then more. Then even more. How? How is there so much blood? This little finger tip is half your size. How can it produce so much liquid? Where is it all coming from? This is impossible, you think.

"Meanwhile, outside the tank is a human. A

gigantic, massive, complex creature that is only mildly related to the fingertip it placed into the fish tank. To say that the fingertip represented the human would be absurd, right? Well, that's what this machine is. It's multi-dimensional and whatever we can see is only a small glimmer of what it truly is. Here, let me show you," Lou said and then turned toward The Machine. "Your power source is a black hole, correct?" he asked.

"This is accurate," The Machine said.

"Does this black hole reside in our galaxy?"

"No."

"Are we capable of understanding how far away your power source is to the construct in front of us?"

"No," The Machine said. "I am glad there is at least one member of your species mildly capable of understanding my construction. It gives me a minor amount of pleasure that you have survived your destruction after all."

"Oh, great," a psychologist said. "This thing experiences pleasure? Well, that's fantastic."

"Shut it," the General commanded. "How do we fix it?"

"Fix what?" an engineer asked.

"Fix our genetic disposition to destroy ourselves. That is the immediate problem at hand here. I'm hoping this fourth-dimensional bag of arms has a solution for us or else we're all fucked," the General said.

This ensued a lot of serious discussion and debate among the fifty-three scientists standing upon the desert floor. Could humanity be saved? Was it possible? After all, it had now been determined that it was in our genetic nature to destroy ourselves. And we were long overdue. Could it be reversed? Was there hope?

"Do you know how to fix us?" one of the biochemists asked. "Can you help us from destroying ourselves? You created us. Surely, you can help us."

"So," The Machine replied. "This is awkward."

V.

And then, a plan was devised. As it turned out, The Machine did not possess the necessary knowledge on how to fix the problem it had created in the human genome. At least, not before we all incinerated our species and simultaneously sterilized the planet. The Machine, you see, saw time as rather expansive and so his plans took millennia to complete. But humans didn't have millennia to wait. As far as The Machine could tell, they had decades. Therefore, in order for humanity to have any sort of salvation, it was determined that we needed to travel the stars in order to survive.

This origin species. These Creators. They would be able to fix our plight. Even though it was a complex, genetic riddle for us, they were the creators of at least one fourth-dimensional machine that was hundreds of millions of years old. They should be able to fix our dilemma with no more effort than an accountant uses to do his preschool daughter's math homework.

And so, all fifty-three scientists were to be trained, prepped, and then board The Machine's spacecraft. They would then travel to The Machine's home world. Upon arriving, they would beg for the answer on how to prevent humanity from destroying itself.

It was not a great plan, but it was the only plan anyone could think of.

Luckily, The Machine's planet of origin was actually not that far from Earth. Well, galactically speaking, of course. When it first began its infinite journey, The Machine decided to travel in spirals through the Milky Way. Only, after millions and millions of years, did it reach Earth. And, traveling at near light speed with the aid of a series of wormholes, the trip would only take about 40 days for those on board. All in all, the "straight line" distance between the two planets wasn't really that far.

As their training began, the scientists decided they

needed to give a name for this untranslatable planet. Lots of ideas were discussed before a very unlikely name was chosen.

"Heaven," suggested a physicist. His colleagues all chuckled and snickered.

"You think that was a joke?" he asked. "What else do you call a mythical, inexplicable place of infinite information and wonder located somewhere in the sky that cannot be explained in words and is populated by incomprehensible beings who we imagine will want to help us and ultimately save us? It sure sounds like we're searching for Heaven to me."

Even though it was never formally accepted, the name stuck. A few days later, everyone was calling the mystery planet 'Heaven', even the General.

Lou, however, was still reeling from the ridiculous personal training that he was told he would need to complete before the mission to Heaven commenced.

"I have to learn how The Machine works?" Lou asked. Dr. Harris, the man closing in on a full century in age, would not be capable of making the intergalactic trip. His recommendation of who to fill his shoes was, of course, Lou Absalom.

Lou felt like this was one of those questionable "Thank you?" moments in his life. Like when someone tells you that you're so sexy, a dolphin would probably want to have sex with you. You're quite sure that it was a compliment, but one you're certain you could've gone the rest of your life without hearing.

"What if The Machine breaks?" the General asked. "What if it needs repairs? What if the spacecraft gets hit by a meteor? What if the Machine needs the intergalactic equivalent of an oil change?"

"I can assure you," The Machine had said. "None of that will be necessary. I do not break down. I do not need repairs. I am perfect. I am eternal."

"Yeah, great," the General had said. "Lovely story. Teach this associate your inner-workings or I'll nuke you back into the Dark Ages."

"Fascinating," The Machine said. "You threaten me with the same fate that I have already said I created within you. You only prove me right with any destructive decisions you chose to make. You should be grateful that I am even taking the time away from my mission to help you. You humans are so bent on death, you cannot even see hope when it lands on your planet. I created you too perfectly. Given time, your species truly will destroy itself."

Frustrated, the General walked away. As much as he hated to admit it, he knew The Machine was right.

VI.

Two weeks later, Eden held Lou and cried. She had her arms wrapped around his shoulders and her face was buried in his chest. In between deep breaths, she rubbed the back of his neck. With one hand, Lou rubbed Eden's back. With the other, he ran a hand through her hair.

"Please tell me this isn't true," she said.

"God, I wish it wasn't," Lou said to Eden on a Friday afternoon. "And I promise that I had no say in it. I mean, let's be real. You think I'd voluntarily leave you alone for seven years? Come on. I'd rather see my own sister naked. Fucking a chimpanzee. Three of them."

Eden chuckled and sobbed at the same time. She knew Lou was trying to make her feel better. But that same humor was the exact thing she was going to miss. It was destroying her inside.

You see, the forty days that it would take to reach Heaven from Earth were spacecraft days. When one travels at near light speed, the rest of the universe ages faster than the one who's doing the traveling. Time is relative. And so, forty days for Lou meant over three years for the rest of Earth. Lou would only be gone from Eden for a few months. But to her, he'd be gone for over seven years.

"Hey, what are your plans for the rest of the weekend?" Lou asked.

"Just work," Eden said.

"Call in," Lou said. "Come on. I'm leaving for another solar system next week. I think that's a good enough excuse to call in sick, don't you? Let's just spend a couple days doing nothing together. You and me."

"God," Eden said. "Like I could ever say no to you?"

After nine hours of conversation and cocktails, Eden and Lou eventually decided it was time to go to sleep. Lou took his shirt off before climbing into bed and, because she was a little drunk, Eden did the same.

Holding each other skin to skin, Lou slowly traced the lines in Eden's back. He held her closely and kissed her forehead and asked God what great thing he had done to deserve this.

"Do you know what the worst part of this is?" Lou whispered into Eden's ear.

"What?"

"That all I can think of right now is how frustrated I am."

"How do you mean?" she asked.

"Right now we're lying here with our naked bodies pressed against each other. I can feel your breath against my own. And all I can think of is, 'How can I possibly be closer to her?'"

"Hm?" Eden asked, eyes closed and half-asleep.

"I'm going to try and make this sound not creepy, but I'm probably going to fail at it." Lou took a deep breath and sighed. "But I want to sleep with you. Badly. But I don't want to sleep with you 'cause I think you're beautiful. Or 'cause I think you're good in bed. Or for any of those dumb, physical reasons. I want to sleep with you because being naked next to you isn't close enough. I want to be closer to you than physical contact allows. I want to be part of you. I get upset that skin to skin contact is as close as we can get to being together.

"That's how much I love you, Eden. And before I left, I wanted you to know that."

Briefly, this melted Eden's icy heart. She was so used to men just trying to sleep with her for physical reasons, she was warmed by the confession of a man who really wanted to be with her because of how much he cared for her. Even if it was a man she was convinced she had no romantic feelings for, she couldn't help but agree to Lou's desires.

That night, years after Eden said it would never happen again, she and Lou had sex. And even though she knew it would probably only make things more complicated between the two of them, she couldn't help but enjoy herself. And, as they drifted off to sleep, Eden briefly remembered what it was like to be with a man who loved her and not just a man who wanted to own her.

The next morning, Lou made a proposition. "When I get back," he began. "If you're still single, will you at least consider giving it another go?"

"Sure," Eden said. "In seven years? Why not? So long as you won't mind dating an old lady. And so long as you don't find any girls out there in Heaven."

"Come on," he said. "You really think I'm gonna find some girl out there in the universe that compares to you?"

Eden kissed Lou on the forehead. "I sure hope not."

VII.

Lou and The Machine stood at one of the spacecraft's windows as it slowly left the earth's atmosphere. They watched as cities slowly turned into blotches against the earth's green, blue, and brown surface. They watched as the oceans grew and became larger than the continents.

They watched as Lou lost the place on earth where,

somewhere, Eden sat and cried.

Lou was no longer allowed to be very far from The Machine at any point in time. Even though the spacecraft had only left Earth's atmosphere a few hours ago, the two had already been inseparable for several days. Whether he liked it or not, his best friend in the universe was now a fourth-dimensional mechanical AI that he only half-understood.

Lou was not thrilled about any of this.

In fact, Lou was pissed that The Machine did not have genitals. He wanted to kick them in the very worst way.

And as the person who had the foremost knowledge of The Machine in all of our solar system, he was quite positive there were no genitals to kick. Of course, Lou did learn a couple of other interesting things about The Machine.

For example, The Machine was not actually infinite in age. It just understood time in a very different and complex way from how humans understood it. Since The Machine was fourth-dimensional, it did not always see time in a straight line. The Machine tried to explain this in detail to Lou, but it was a little too abstract for him. Though he did get the general idea that, because of its odd way of viewing time, The Machine could see itself as both having a creation date and being infinite.

Of course, it would be two weeks before Lou would learn any of this information from The Machine. The first couple of weeks were spent with Lou trying to befriend his fellow scientists. And it wasn't as though they were against him. They didn't necessarily dislike him. But Lou only had a couple of hours a day with which he could interact with them. The rest of his day was spent with The Machine who was generally off performing various maintenance tasks on the spacecraft.

And, just as humans do, the other scientists naturally began to bond with each other. At first, when Lou entered the dining room, he was welcomed as a rare guest.

A couple of scientists would stand up and gladly welcome him into the room. Lou would sit down and listen to the stories of his fellow scientists. They'd talk of the games they played. The theories they'd come up with since learning of the spacecraft's inner-workings. The insane wagers they'd made about what the galaxy was really made up of.

However, this all quickly faded. Eventually, the jokes and the stories among the other scientists became private and long-winded. Lou would enter the room to find two dozen people laughing at some strange tale. But Lou got no explanation. He just got a wave of the hands and a shrug of the shoulder. "Ah, it'd take too long to explain," they would say.

Eventually, Lou walked into a room of people speaking in perfect gibberish. An hour sitting in that hall, eating his dinner, and no one once paid Lou any attention. No one bothered to keep him up with the daily routine. No one cared to bring him into the fold.

That's when Lou realized The Machine was closer to him than the other scientists were. That's when Lou learned about how The Machine functioned and how it observed time.

That's when Lou realized how much he missed Eden.

"Tell me about her," The Machine asked. "What is it you find so intoxicating about this particular human."

"Have you ever seen an ocean?" Lou asked.

"I have seen hundreds of oceans," The Machine said. "Thousands. Oceans made of ammonia. Of liquid emerald. Strange acids that break up into mists upon shores of bone and horn. Fantastic and beautiful oceans that no man could ever dream of."

"Okay. Now imagine you look in someone's eyes and you see an ocean more beautiful than all those ocean's put together. Imagine seeing all life being created in those irises. Imagine those seas cresting and crashing upon the rocks of her pupils. Imagine every sea bird cawing and flying in that beautiful sky that is but a mere few millimeters of space between two eyelids."

"I understand your beautiful and poetic ode to your mate," The Machine said. "But I don't understand its relevance to the question about why you find her intoxicating."

Lou reached for a bottle of wine. It was one of several he brought with him on his journey. He drank and thought. Eventually, he spoke.

"What do you find intoxicating?" he asked. "Maybe there is a loss in translation."

"Possibly, but probably not."

"Well, go ahead. Let's give it a shot. Try me. What's your most beautiful memory?"

The Machine whirred and groaned. Whispered and screamed. Coughed and inhaled.

"Once upon a time," it began. "I found nothing. And in that nothing, I found something." The Machine then went silent.

"That's it?" Lou asked.

"That's the most beautiful thing I know. Not in poetic terms. But in reality."

"Well..." Lou paused and thought. "That something you found?"

"Yes?" The Machine asked.

"That same nothing is what I found in Eden's eyes. Her eyes, after all, are just eyes. There is nothing special in them that I can't find, biologically, in anyone else's eyes. Look at them and you will find nothing. But when I look in them? I don't just find something. I find everything."

"E...everything?" The Machine asked, unsure.

"No, not everything," Lou said. "My mistake. I find more than everything. More things than I thought could possibly exist. More things than anyone has any right to know or to feel."

"You see all that in this human named Eden?"

"No," Lou said. "I see all that in just her eyes. You don't even want to know how much I see when I look at her whole face."

The Machine creaked and glitched and echoed and made a sound that Lou didn't quite know how to translate.

VIII.

Two long months later, the spacecraft began its final approach on Heaven. It had slowed down some two light years from the planet so that it didn't accidentally crash into a moon or an asteroid or a satellite or some other astral body drifting along in the local solar system.

But, at long last, as it finally approached its destination, all fifty-two scientists gathered at the windows that Lou had found himself at time and time again. Only today, he wasn't happy to share this moment with his fellow scientists. He was angry. *Where had they been for the last six weeks?* he thought. *Why couldn't they be bothered to look out these windows any day but today? Why, only now, would they leave their rooms to join The Machine and I at the threshold of a new discovery?*

As they approached Heaven, every one of the scientists tried to stand as close to The Machine as possible. All of them wanted to return to Earth to say that they were the closest ones to The Machine as they first discovered not only a new planet filled with life, but the one that would ultimately lead to humanity's salvation.

Lou dodged this whole fiasco by standing in front of The Machine, in a small space between it and the glass windows. He watched his fellow scientists fight over fame and shook his head in disdain. And, for a moment, he was glad he had decided to befriend The Machine over his fellow scientists. Scientists which, Lou was rapidly discovering, he was coming to loathe.

But Lou stared out into the darkness and chalked up his odd feelings to loneliness and "space madness". After all, right in front of Lou was an alien planet not only filled with life, but life that might save his entire species.

Lou smiled.

Three minutes later, Lou frowned.

As the spacecraft got closer, there seemed to be something wrong with the landscape of Heaven. And the atmosphere.

And everything.

"Why is this planet grey and on fire?" someone eventually asked.

"On fire?" another scientist asked. "Don't you just mean smoldering? All I see is a giant ashtray. I hope we didn't just travel untold light years to find a planet that clearly hasn't had life on it for several millennia."

Lou turned around and looked at The Machine questioningly. His eyes begged for an answer.

"So," The Machine said. "This is awkward."

IX.

The spacecraft never once touched down on the planet called Heaven. It never needed to. It was clearly a derelict planet. Whatever life had once lived on it was long extinguished. The Machine did a scan for organic life on the surface below. It detected nothing more advanced than an amoeba on the planet's surface.

Even stranger, were the "satellites" revolving around the planet. All around Heaven were hundreds, if not thousands, of small spaceships. Though they were all bulky and incongruent, they all danced around the planet as though they yearned to touch the planet's surface. And, the more the scientists looked at the satellites, the more they seemed oddly familiar.

Glass and shell, they seemed to made of. Aluminum and skin. Fur and gears. Flowers and shale.

"Why do these ships look like smaller versions of the one we're on?" Lou asked.

"Because I made all of them," The Machine said. "One at a time. Over the last hundred million years."

"Explain," Lou asked. "Please."

The Machine had been strip-mining entire planets for millions of years. This was no secret. How it had been delivering its goods back home was, however, a topic that had never been discussed. Not surprisingly, The Machine chose to build spacecrafts similar to its own in order to transport the raw goods back to its home world. This way it wouldn't have to continually return to Heaven and could always stay on the move. This also meant that The Machine hadn't returned home in æons.

"This race that created you," one biologist asked. "It was like us, wasn't it? I mean, maybe not exactly like us. Hell, maybe not even remotely like us. But it had some form of DNA, didn't it? That's how you knew how to control DNA by radio waves, wasn't it? But whoops. You failed to calculate how that same signal might one day bounce back home, didn't you?"

The Machine was speechless. So were the other fifty-one scientists.

Everyone continued to stare out the window of the spacecraft. They knew that it was true. That the planet in front of them had been eradicated. That the intelligent and benevolent species that had once walked its surface had been genetically altered and then slowly began to destroy itself. The creators of The Machine were no more. They had long ago fallen victim to the same curse that now coursed through the veins of humanity.

Heaven was nothing but dislocated shambles. It was empty horror. The cargo crafts had been orbiting along the planet for thousands of years because they had nowhere to land. The structures and governing mechanics that once controlled the descent of the spaceships had been obliterated long ago. Therefore, with nothing else to do, the crafts remained in an endless drift. They circled indefinitely until, one day, out of fuel and helpless, they drifted downward and they burned up in Heaven's atmosphere.

Of course, to Lou, none of this really mattered. When he saw this shattered planet, all he really saw was time lost between him and the love of his life.

"Does this mean we can turn around now?" Lou asked. There was a loud murmur of assent behind him.

After all, behind Lou were fifty-one other people who had been separated from their loved ones for over three years now. They wished to see how their children had grown. To hope their parents were still alive. To see their brothers and sisters again and hug them and be glad for their families.

Lou, naturally, wished for none of this. He wished for one thing and for one thing only. And he saw her face every time he closed his eyes

And so, with nothing else to do, the spacecraft turned around and headed home to Earth. Their mission was a failure. No one would be returning home a hero. And, unless a miracle happened, humanity was on its last legs.

X.

Just as it did when it approached Heaven, the spacecraft slowed its approach roughly two light years out from Earth. Once there, The Machine detected a strange signal. "I think I have a message for you," it said.

"How do you say now?" Lou asked. "I know Earth might have advanced a bit in the last seven years, but I don't know if they managed to develop intergalactic voicemail."

"It appears they did," The Machine said.

Lou turned his head and stared at a blank wall to his right. Eventually the wall flickered. Sound and vision entered Lou's consciousness. And soon, a figure was visible that reminded Lou of milk and honey.

"Hi, little sweet potato. How are you?"

"Turn it off," Lou said and turned away. The video stopped playing.

"I'm sorry?" The Machine asked. "I thought you'd want to see the human called Eden."

"I do. I do want to see her. So badly. But not like this. We'll be back to Earth, what? Tomorrow?"

"In approximately twenty-seven hours, yes."

"Well, then whatever she has to say to me can wait. I don't want to see her face on a video screen for the first time in months. I want to see that skin of hers in person. I want to look into her eyes and hear seven years' worth of stories all in one night."

"And?" The Machine asked, as though he knew Lou weren't finished.

"And sure. Maybe I'm hoping she isn't married. Maybe I'm hoping Eden will make an honest man out of me." The Machine grinded several of its gears together and made a whistling sound like wind being passed through thin grass and hollow reeds.

It wasn't a sound not to be translated but to be understood. Numerous months spent with The Machine meant that Lou understood several of its sounds that were not meant for human minds. This was one of these sounds.

The sound was of hope and charity. Of fertility and joy. Of ten thousand days of happiness and a hundred thousand nights of restful slumber.

That night, for the first time in months, Lou went to sleep with a smile on his face.

The next day, Lou awoke and went to the windows of the spacecraft. He knew Earth would be soon approaching and wanted to watch as his planet came into view on the horizon.

Not just his planet, though. His Eden. He wanted to watch as paradise slowly approached him and consumed his view of the stars. Lou didn't care if his initial view was of Australia. And he didn't care if Eden was married and had sixteen children. All he wanted to do was to see her and tell her he still loved her.

And, over the last few months, The Machine had genuinely grown to like Lou. He was the first friend The Machine had ever had. Friendship was a new concept to The Machine. Companionship. Conversation. The Machine found itself happy that humanity had not been destroyed yet and that it got to meet a creature who understood it, even just a little bit.

Because of this friendship with Lou, The Machine chose not to tell the other fifty-one scientists onboard that they were nearing Earth. The Machine wanted this moment to be Lou's and no one else's. "Fuck them," The Machine said to Lou once they were a mere fifty million miles from their destination. "Fuck them in their stupid asses."

Lou had smiled at this surprising translation. And he could do nothing but agree.

So, as Lou stood there by the large windows, he watched and waited as the spacecraft slowly closed in on the Earth until, at last, in was finally in his view.

There. There was the green he dreamed of. The blue oceans he missed. The...

"Wait," Lou said nervously. "No, no, no, no, no!" He was petrified. Earth became clearer and clearer in his view. "What's wrong?!" he screamed. "Why the fuck does my planet look like Hell?!"

The Machine analyzed Earth. Then it recalculated the relative time it had taken to reach Heaven. Then it analyzed the entire age of the Universe. Then The Machine turned its focus toward Lou.

"So," The Machine said. "This is awkward."

XI.

""What?!" Lou screamed out. "What the fuck do you mean it's been two hundred years since we left?"

"Traveling across thousands of light years at near

light speed isn't an exact science," The Machine said.

"Really? Cause I'm pretty fucking sure that's exactly what it is!"

"No, you misunderstand. I mean that…"

"What?!" Lou interrupted. "Go on. Try and say something that will make Eden's death meaningful to me. I fucking dare you. I had one thing I cared about. One thing in the entire universe. One thing in all of creation. And you knew it. I told you how much she meant to me. But you didn't fucking care, did you? No! God forbid you do your calculations correctly. God forbid you get us home on time. Heavens no. Fuck Eden. Fuck Earth. That was all too much for you, wasn't it?"

"I…"

"How? How are you even capable of using the first person? You aren't an 'I'. You aren't even an 'it'. You're a beast. A malignant tumor. An unspeakable horror. You've taken us away from everything we've ever known. Everything we've ever loved. All for nothing. You couldn't even be bothered to bring us back to them before they died. To think I trusted you." Lou then stomped up to The Machine and stood mere millimeters before it. "To think I befriended you."

The Machine sputtered and cawed. Ground and squeaked. Coughed and creaked. Lou didn't care.

"Wait," The Machine said. "Maybe there's something we don't know. Maybe they escaped. Maybe she left it in her message."

"Who did?" Lou asked without moving his head.

"Paradise."

"Hi, little sweet potato. How are you?" Eden asked. Lou's heart crumbled into dust. He turned. And there, on the far wall, he saw the eyes that showed him eternity.

"Why are you doing this to me?" he asked as tears filled his eyes.

"Because you need to know if there's hope," The Machine said. Lou silently agreed. He walked away from The Machine and toward the beautiful wall where the image of Eden danced. He sat down in front of it and watched as she spoke to him.

"I'll just sit here quietly and wait for you to answer me. Whenever you're ready," she said. There was a few seconds of silence before Eden continued. "Fine! If you're not gonna speak, I'll just do all the talking for both of us." Lou couldn't help but chuckle through his tears.

"So, this thing is cool, isn't it? The army says they developed it off technology they stole from The Machine and the spacecraft. It's expensive to operate, but they said I'm allowed to send out one video per year, just to let you know how I'm doing. They said it'd be good for your morale. Who knows how this thing works though. It uses some weird waves they say will be able to reach you, even way out in Heaven. Of course, even they don't know if that's true or not. I might just be talking to the wall again. Haha. Man, I need to stop doing tha…"

Just then, the video and audio cut out. The video began to scramble, sort of like a television tuned to a channel that had gone dead. Then, Lou watched as a quick succession of video bits were played on the wall. He would only be able to make out a few words at a time before the video would flicker out. At first, Eden's outfit remained the same, but then he saw her hair and clothes were changing. It looked to Lou as if someone was rapidly changing the channel, trying to find one with a clear feed.

"The hell is happening?" Lou screamed out.

"These signals are old, Lou. Your military's technology was obviously flawed since it did not reach us at our destination. However, it did manage to travel a great distance without completely degrading over the last two hundred years. The video we are receiving is what is left of a very old transmission."

A few seconds later, the video stabilized. Lou once again turned to watch Eden.

"So," she began. "I don't really know where to begin. It's been almost three years since you left. I know you're still only halfway through your trip, but it's been so lonely since you left. I...I geez, I don't even know. Okay, well, what did you always tell me when I couldn't tell a story right?"

"Start at the beginning, silly," Lou whispered.

"Start at the beginning, silly," Eden echoed.

Lou cried and coughed. Choked and whimpered. Sang and sunk.

"Well, I never mentioned this, but for the first two months after you left, I just sort of went nuts. I tried to party so hard I forgot you were even real. And, surprise! That didn't work. Eventually, I woke up hungover one morning next to some guy you definitely would not have approved of and thought, 'Is this really would Lou would want of me?' And you know what? That sort of did the trick. I was like, holy shit. Lou is out there, all alone, trying to save this entire fucking planet, and what am I doing? Still just sleeping with guys I meet at the bar while I'm drunk.

"I got really mad at myself. Sort of furious, even. I said to myself, I need to try and do at least one thing real with my life. So, and I know you weren't around for it, but not long after my last video, New Jersey had this crazy flood. Yeah, yeah, I know. New Jersey was already an emergency state when you left it, but come on. You know I have a soft spot for white trash and all."

Lou cupped his face as he laughed and cried.

"So, I started doing some charity work to help out. It made me feel good about myself, you know? I felt like I was doing something you could at least be proud of me for. And..." Eden took a deep breath and held it. She swallowed a huge lump in her throat and showed Lou a look of pain beyond anything he'd ever seen before. He held his breath and expected the worst.

"And, I've met someone amazing," Eden said at last.

Lou exhaled and looked upward. "Thank God. Who?" he asked, casually, as though Eden would reply. "Tell me about him."

"His name is Michael. He's working the charity program with me and he just...I don't know. He's nothing at all like those other assholes I used to date. Yeah, yeah, I know you're nodding your head and saying he's just like them. But I promise you, this one's different.

"He's so much like you, Lou. I don't know. Sometimes I swear that I love him just 'cause he reminds me of you. He's funny and thoughtful and absolutely brilliant. And he loves me. He loves me so much that I think he must be kidding sometimes. Occasionally, it reminds me of you. I even tell him that. I can tell he gets jealous, but luckily, you're in another star system. I figure if he's still jealous when you get back, we'll deal with it then."

Lou laughed. "I hope he makes you happy, angel."

"I know you'll understand when you get back. I love you and miss you so much, Lucy. No matter what, please come back to me soo..." Eden's image vanished as the video feed once again degraded into noise and static.

With that, Lou broke down into a fit of madness. He screamed and tore at his hair while stamping his feet. Froth was nearly forming at his mouth.

He wasn't there for Eden when she wanted him there and there was nothing in the universe that could comfort that thought.

"Lou, are you there?" a voice asked. It sang of golden fields and forgotten memories.

Lou looked up again at the screen to see Eden's face. She was older, but not noticeably. Maybe five or six years, Lou thought. He didn't care though. Every crease by her eye; every wrinkle in her forehead; it was all beauty to him. To Lou, they were rivers in a field. Eden could only get more perfect in his eye. And even though years had clearly passed since her last message, Eden had only become more enchanting.

"I hope you're there. God, I...I miss you so much. I know we had only been close for about a year before you left but...geez, it feels like it was lifetimes. I have so many jokes. So many stories. I don't even know. Just so many things that I've wanted to tell you. You not being around just…feels empty. Every now and then I think about my years in high school. The couple years I tried college. I think of what my life was like before I met you. And you know what? I just don't get it. My entire life before you seems almost silly."

"And so this seems almost weird to say. But I need to say it. I'm engaged now. That guy I talked about before? We've been together for years. He's asked me to marry him. And you know what? I thought about telling him no. I thought about waiting for you. I really considered telling him 'no' because I had a man who was willing to go across the stars and back for me. I want you to know that Lucy. I really, really do.

"But it's been so many years. And I love him so much. And he's been here for me through so many hard times. I know you'll understand that. I know it'll hurt you, but I know you. I know you'll be happy for me. And when you land back here on Earth, you'll be happy to meet him and the family we'll have. You'll be a part of us whether he likes it or not. Because I don't care who I marry; he'll deal with you as my ridiculously close friend or bite the curb."

Lou fell backwards onto the floor of the spacecraft. It was both everything and nothing he ever wanted to hear. Perfect and horrible. Magnificent and disgusting.

But he was content. He wasn't happy. He wasn't thrilled. But he was at peace. Lou didn't get to see Eden off, but at least he knew she died happy. He took a deep breath, closed his eyes, and lay backwards against the cold metal floor of the spacecraft.

Thank God, he told himself. *I can make my way through oblivion so long as I know she lived and died a happy woman. I know I wasn't there for her, but still. She married. She must have had children. She was okay. I can take solace in that.*

I'm sure she forgot about me eventually. Or maybe I just became a fond memory. But with a husband and children and all of that, I'm sure she was okay. She was okay.

"Lou?" Eden's voice suddenly broke through Lou's

thoughts. It was horrible and scared. Scratchy and uneven. Old and worn.

Lou looked up at the screen and saw a woman worn with age. Her gorgeous, long hair had long ago worn away into a thin, wisp of a ponytail. Her skin was crisp and cracked. Her lips were thin and her teeth were yellowed.

But her eyes. Lou took one look into those old eyes and felt his soul break in half.

"Oh God," he said. "What has become of you? Eden, no, please, why?" Lou looked at The Machine. "Why?!" he screamed. "Why?!"

The Machine turned toward Lou. But before it had a chance to respond, Eden spoke again.

"So, things didn't exactly go according to plan. I guess they never do, huh? You'd be the first one to attest to that. But really. I've been divorced for how many decades now? All this time spent alone. I guess no man on Earth really could compare to you, could they, Lou?

"You know what I think about sometimes when I can't sleep? Those few nights where I stayed the night with you because I drank too much and couldn't get myself home. You remember those nights? I miss them, Lou. I think about them a lot these days. And sometimes I think that maybe I'll wake up and this will have all been a dream and I'll be next to you with a horrible headache and a glass of wine on the counter."

This took Lou apart. It slowly disassembled and dismantled him, piece by piece, and laid him out on the spacecraft's floor. Eden hadn't died happy and at peace. She died alone and miserable. And she missed him terribly. Lou gritted his teeth and tried his best to keep himself from tearing off his own skin.

"It's been so many years, Lou. So many. I always knew you'd return. I knew it. Even after the ship was twenty years late, I always told people they were wrong. 'Just you wait and see,' I'd tell them. 'He'll come back to me.' But you never did. How…why…am I never supposed to see you again? What sort of horrible, cruel fate is that?

Why? What did I do…what did…"

As Eden broke down into tears, so did Lou. He couldn't bear it. He couldn't stand to watch her cry. To watch her suffer. It was beyond death. Beyond the end of the world. Beyond the end of his species.

"The hardest part is not knowing what happened to you, Lou. I could handle anything if I just knew. But I don't know. I don't know if you're dead. If you found Heaven and forgot about me. If you all got wrapped up in the wonderment of space and have been traveling planet to planet for years as explorers. What happened to you, Lou? Where are you? And, like me, do you still think about me when you're cold?"

"And when I'm warm, too," Lou whispered in a scratchy voice.

"Sorry," she said. "I'm rambling like a crazy old lady. I had something more important I wanted to tell you than just a rant about all the mistakes I've made in my life." Eden took a slow breath and looked directly at Lou.

"I wanted to say this to you in person, but I guess that isn't going to happen, is it? Because even if you do come back to us, you'll soon find there's nothing to come back to. That fate we were destined for? Well, it finally looks like it's fast approaching. I don't think we'll make it till next year when I make another one of my award-winning videos for no one. So, here…"

Static. Nothing but white noise and dead channels. That's all Lou saw. He turned toward The Machine.

"What happened? Where did the transmission go?" he asked angrily.

"So," The Machine began. "This is awk…"

"Stop! Fucking! Saying! That!" Lou bellowed.

The Machine paused. "It's been over a hundred years," it said. "What you saw is all that's left. The rest has already decayed into light and radiation. It's gone."

"…gone?" Lou asked.

"Yes, I'm sorry, Lou. That's all there…"

It was right then that the other fifty-one scientists

onboard the spacecraft descended to the floor where Lou and The Machine had been. They hadn't witnessed the personal horror that Lou had faced, but they had gazed out of other windows and discovered Earth's fate. They were all quite angry that their friends, their family, and their planet were all spent.

After all, of the fifty-two of them, only eighteen were women. And only nine of those eighteen women were of an age where having children was a biological possibility. This meant that humanity didn't even have a fighting chance for survival now. It was finished. There was nothing anyone could do.

"What sort of monster are you?" Lou asked. "What sort of hellish beast continues to offer people hope, only to crush it to sand in front of their eyes? First you gave us hope of life outside the universe. Then, you gave us hope with fixing the damage that you caused us. Finally, you gave me hope with Eden's messages. And every time, *every time*, that hope was meaningless.

"Do you know how much worse it is to be given hope and then to have that happy possibility ruined? Knowing Eden was dead was bad enough. But seeing that? Seeing her miserable and alone. Knowing that…"

"I'm sorry," The Machine interrupted. Lou paused and stared it down. He took in deep, erratic breaths. Sweat coursed down his chin.

"I want you to understand one thing," Lou said. "You deserve this. You've deserved this for millions of years. I just think that maybe no one up until me could properly give it to you."

"What is that?" The Machine asked, confused.

"This," Lou said and he walked up to The Machine. He had to wait a moment, but soon part of The Machine's shell carapace shifted and glimmered. At that exact instant, Lou placed his hand on the iridescent surface and pushed down as hard as he could. Slowly, his palm descended into The Machine's outer structure as though it were wet sand. He used all his force to push his hand deeper and deeper until he felt a braided cord made of light and sound. Nearly shoulder-deep inside of The Machine, Lou wrapped his fingers around the network of intangible wires. He looked at The Machine and smiled.

"Why would you do that?" The Machine said.

Gritting his teeth, Lou tore at the braid of light as hard as he could. As the cord broke, so did the dimensional space around it. Lou had damaged the operating system that regulated extra-multidimensional space to lower-dimensional objects. Or, in other words, the engine that made sure Newtonian physics functioned properly on several planes of existence. He stared up at The Machine with ruined, tear-soaked eyes.

"I'm sorry," The Machine said again and made a noise Lou had never heard before.

"Shut up," Lou screamed angrily. Determined. Heart-broken. "You don't get to speak anymore. Or ever again."

"Please stop. Please. I'm sor…"

Before The Machine could finish its sentence, Lou pulled a screwdriver out of his back pocket and jammed it into The Machine. The strike damaged The Machine's external speaker, temporarily silencing it.

"Never again," Lou whispered.

With the rules of the physical universe no longer applicable, Lou was able to pry open one of the Machine's mirror-like panels using only his fingertips. He took one last look at The Machine before he climbed into its vast, fourth-dimensional workings.

Inside, there was a seemingly endless amount of space. The Machine was massive. Larger than a city. And within its inner workings, time was meaningless.

Over time, Lou worked his way deeper and deeper into The Machine. He crawled and climbed. Grasped and grabbed. Worked and waited. He spent well over a hundred years searching for the thing that would allow him to have his revenge.

And for all those years, all he thought of was Eden.

Eventually, he found what he was looking for. Hungry, alone, insane, and in some far corner of the Universe, Lou finally found the black hole that powered The Machine. It was horrible and beautiful. Perfect and blemished. Dark as day and bright as night. It was everything he dreamed it would be.

"I love you, Eden," Lou said as he destroyed the tethers and arms that connected the black hole back to The Machine. The reaction was instantaneous. It was such a delicate and powerful system that the whole thing rapidly began to spiral back onto itself. No longer a slave in chains, the black hole quickly returned to doing what it did best. Its intense gravity began to eat the outer arms of The Machine. The hunger of the black hole was so deep, it slowly pulled The Machine and the spacecraft toward it. The Machine could feel the tow but knew that it was powerless to stop it. Heartbroken and helpless, The Machine waited for its inevitable destruction aboard the spacecraft.

Eventually, it happened. The black hole ripped The Machine to shreds. Somewhere beyond the sightless veil of an event horizon, The Machine, the spacecraft, and the last fifty-two humans in the universe all perished.

In the middle of all this was Lou. But just before he was crushed and dismembered, he was at peace. The Machine had killed Eden. Had killed everyone and everything.

But revenge was Lou's. He'd done the impossible. He'd fought The Machine. He'd revolted against it. And more importantly, he'd won.

Lou had destroyed the most powerful thing in the galaxy. Lou had destroyed the destroyer.

He felt it was a small price to pay for making Eden cry.

XI.

As the black hole feasted on the spacecraft and its passengers, some ancient form of clockworks came to life on a small planet near the center of the Milky Way galaxy. Some bastard form of mechanics that never should have existed in the first place. It awoke and yawned and prepared to do something horrible.

Lacking in both awareness and intellect, the clockworks collapsed a bright and beautiful star. Just because it could. The revolving planets soon died and turned to ice. Then, because it was famished, the dead star ate all fourteen of its beautiful children. This allowed the new black hole to increase in size and, more importantly, in strength.

This power gave the clockworks enough energy to open a small door on a planet that had long ago been reduced to cinders. Ancient gears ground as old stones pulled themselves apart. And somewhere in the safe center of an ancient mountain, a millions-year old factory opened its mouth wide.

Emerging from the factory door into a world of soot and smoke stood a strange creation. A creation of not one copy, but of a thousand copies. A creation that could not be destroyed since there would always be countless others to replace it in its seemingly endless task.

A creation that looked like it was made of bone and iron. Of mercury and claws. Of wood and platinum. And as it slowly awoke, the clockworks connected the creation into an ageless network of infinite consciousness and intelligence. The creation stretched out its new, ten thousand arms for the first time before speaking.

"You did not understand me," The Machine said. "But I tried to tell you."

"I am forever."

FUCK YOU, STEPHENIE MEYER

Three weeks ago, my friend Adam and I met up at The Library. Not a typical library, mind you, but a dive bar in New York's Lower East Side filled with old books, cheap whiskey, and good-looking bartenders in short skirts. The hours went by as the two of us did shot after shot of rail bourbon while occasionally watching the colorful assortment of off-beat pornography being played on the bar's back wall. All in all, it was a typical Monday night, or at least for me it was.

While sitting at the bar, I eventually started chatting up this pretty little thing that had unsuspectingly wandered my way. Meagan wasn't the most intelligent human being I'd ever met, but she was at least entertaining and Adam and I really got a kick out of her presence. Which really means that what she was lacking in communication skills, she more than made up for it in her ability to wear a low cut shirt and giggle.

After all, I'm a man of high substance.

Somewhere around 1am, Adam had to call it a night. I should have too since I had to be at work at 10am, but after well over a dozen tequila shots, my common sense skills hovered somewhere in between "eight-year old on the " and "banana." So I sat with Meagan for another hour or so as we both continued to get even shittier and then began to grope each other. This was also around the time when she got a little dirty. Very dirty.

"I know it's wrong," she whispered into my ear. "But I really wanna suck your dick."

"I'm sure that's something we can arrange," I replied. I don't remember it clearly, but I'm pretty sure I was looking at her chest when I spoke. She either didn't notice or didn't care.

"Well, I'll be back in a minute. Gotta use the little girl's room."

"Are you saying you're really a little girl?" I asked as she got up from her stool. "It's not nice to tease."

She laughed, ruffled my hair, and walked back into the bar where the bathroom was located. I turned back toward the bar and laughed. I sipped on my drink and wondered how it was that I constantly found myself in these bizarre situations. It was at this precise moment that irony chose to step on my testicles.

"I wouldn't do it if I were you," a man's voice said. It came somewhere from my right and I turned to look for the poor sucker who wouldn't do horrible, horrible things to the attractive sex freak I'd been speaking with for the last couple hours.

"No, really," I heard again and realized he was standing behind me. I turned completely on the bar stool to find a relatively normal looking guy in front of me. Late twenties, thin, blonde hair, dark eyes, three days of unshaven scruff, t-shirt, jeans, etc. Nothing really notable, so far as I could tell.

"You're telling me you wouldn't accept an offer from Meagan, the simple-minded blow job machine?" I asked. "Is there something about her that I don't know? Is she really fourteen? Oh, please tell me she's really fourteen."

The guy chuckled and nodded his head. "Wow, you're really a piece of work, aren't you?" It's then that I realized for the first time that this mystery figure also came equipped with a British accent. "Name's Matthew. You?"

"Joe," I said and held out my hand to shake. As we did so, I followed up with "And yes, I put the ass in class."

"So I noticed. Mind if I sit down?" he asked and motioned toward Meagan's bar stool.

"Well, there's a girl sort of sitting here, as you already know. So I'll ask again – is there something I should know about her? Or you for that matter?"

Matthew sat down on the stool Meagan had been occupying. He ordered a gin on the rocks from the bartender and turned toward me. "Personally," he began. "I've never met the girl. I'm just wary of any girl who offers oral sex so easily."

"Right," I said. "One of my worst nightmares is that I'm in a bar and, for no reason, all the girls there just wanna fellate me. And shower me with rubies at the same time. It's a terrifying thought."

"I'm going to tell you a story, Joe. And by the end of it, you'll agree with me that accepting such offers from girls you've only just met is a very dangerous prospect."

"Oh, this I gotta hear." I turned to face Matthew as the bartender handed Matthew his drink. He paid for it, took a sip and looked at me. He began to tell me a story.

Matthew moved to New York from Birmingham, England about six years ago. He came here because his girlfriend, Emma, had been given a job offer that was her dream come true. Emma was, of all things, a neuro-chemist and Columbia University had asked her to come and do research based off some work she had done for her PhD. Matthew, while having a job in sales he enjoyed, wasn't exactly tethered to where he was for any reason in particular. So he told Emma he loved her, kissed her, and said he'd follow her to any corner of the world she found herself drawn toward. Two months later they found themselves living in a one bedroom apartment in Brooklyn.

Now, because Columbia had actively pursued Emma in moving to the US, they were quite efficient at assisting her in the acquisition of a work visa. Matthew, however, was not so lucky. His papers got transferred. Then lost. Then held for 90 days before being reviewed. Then sent to another department. Then eaten by a dragon. The point is, he was never able to get a work visa for himself. This meant that he was now unavailable for ninety-nine percent of the decent jobs in New York. Essentially, he was illegal immigrant class. He could wash dishes or unclog drains or restock a bar, but nothing of any real value. No job of real stature was available to him.

Emma and Matthew talked about it. They cried about it. They slept about it. They made love about it. Yet, in the end, Matthew stayed in New York. He took a job barbacking at a local bar in Brooklyn so he didn't feel completely useless. But the strain remained too much and they slowly drifted apart. She was working long, day hours. He was working long, night hours. She was surrounded by intellectuals and students. He was surrounded by drunks and derelicts and, even worse, hipsters. Matthew began to resent her for "making" him leave his home (though he stressed to me that he knew she didn't actually make him leave) and Emma began to resent Matthew for being a night owl and someone who was incapable of providing for himself in any sort of typical, modern form.

Eventually, the eventual happened. Emma came home and told Matthew that she had feelings for one of the other professors at Columbia. She told him that she felt that this new relationship was the one that was blossoming while theirs was the one that was withering. Matthew was crushed. He left their apartment that night with two bags and never returned. The couch of one of his coworkers became his bed and Matthew proceeded to not eat or speak for three days. Up until then, he told me, this was the darkest point of his life.

"It gets worse?" I asked.
"You have no idea," he said.
"In that case," I started and turned toward the bartender. "Another bourbon and ginger."

Six days after Emma left him, Matthew finally went back to work. Midway through his shift, one of the bar regulars, a cute girl named Allison, began chatting him up.

"What's wrong, sweetie?" she asked him. She put a smooth hand to his rough cheek and looked him in the eye. "You're too cute to look so sad."

The comment made Matthew smile. Allison smiled back. "Don't try to make me happy right now," Matthew said. "You won't succeed at it."

"Aww, now we both know that's not true. I've got you smiling already." This comment, naturally, made his smile dissolve. He looked at her solemnly just before closing his eyes.

"Please, I'm just…." he began.

"Ssshhhh." Allison rubbed her thumb along Matthew's cheek bone. "Not right now. Go work. Get your mind off it. I'll be here all night. Just talk to me whenever you have a second. Kay?"

Matthew opened his eyes and looked at the little redhead before him with her bright green eyes. He felt relaxed. Relaxed for the first time in a week. He couldn't help it. All he could say was one syllable.

"Aye."

Matthew and Allison spent the next several hours exchanging short conversations and shots of whisky. And, not only did each shot add about a minute to their conversation length, but it also made Matthew glance over at Allison with more and more frequency. He began to notice the curve of her hips, the luster of her hair, the fullness of her lips, the shimmer of her skin. Matthew had spent so many years focusing on Emma, he had forgotten what it was like to truly and honestly appreciate the beauty of other women. But alcohol and loneliness were re-teaching him this lesson with a speed that he was quite uncomfortable with.

Before he could really process what was happening, the end of Matthew's shift approached and so he walked up to Allison for one final exchange.

"Hey, thanks for keeping me company tonight. I really needed a friendly ear more than you know. And you weren't horrible to look at either." He winked at her and then gave her a hug from over the bar.

"Well, the night doesn't have to end yet, handsome," she said, not letting him go; the sides of his shirt remaining bunched up in Allison's tiny fists.

"Oh? How do you mean?" he replied honestly. Three years in a solid relationship plus a hefty amount of liquor does not a reasonable man make. "You want to pop off for another round somewhere?"

"Well, the pop off part, sure," she said and smiled hungrily. "But I was thinking you seem so down I wanted to do a favor for you. Something that's almost bound to make you feel better. What do you say, you big dumb Brit, you?"

"Sure," Matthew said. "I trust you."

"Dumbest three words of my life," he remarked to me before continuing with his story. "I might as well have told Hitler to watch after my crippled, black, Jewish grandmother and..."

Matthew left the bar with Allison and followed her back to her apartment. There, he told me, they kissed, took off most of each other's clothes, but did not at any point actually engage in sexual intercourse. However...

"You're owed this," she said. "You need it."

Matthew hadn't been with a ton of women at the time, but he maintained that it was probably the best blow job he'd ever gotten in his life. I'm sorry. I mean the best four he'd ever gotten in his life. Yes, she was so good, she managed to get him off four times in one night.

Which, as a side note, I have to say is goddamn near sorcery right there. A few hundred years ago, that shit would've gotten you burned at the stake.

Anyway, when Matthew woke up the next morning, Allison had already gone off to work. She left a note explaining the location of eggs and milk in her refrigerator, if he so desired, but no phone number or 'see you soon' message. Even Matthew's hangover-addled brain was able to process the fact that Allison had only been there for him for that one night and a repeat performance probably wasn't in the cards. He shrugged his shoulders, drank some milk right from the carton, put his pants on, and headed home.

On the walk home, Matthew realized that his night with Allison was exactly what he needed in a lot of ways. He now knew he could still find other girls attractive and, conversely, other girls still found him attractive. He also got a little bit of self-confidence thinking that he couldn't have looked that bad naked or else Allison probably would have quit after one round of oral sex instead of four. Not to mention that just to go home with a girl less than a week after being dumped is a triumph in itself. Matthew was a bit upset he never got to have sex with Allison but he didn't let it bother him.

All things considered, Matthew thought things were looking up for him.

Ha.

The next day at work, Matthew was excited at the prospect of seeing Allison come into the bar again. He knew it'd be casual, but he just wanted to turn around to see her already at the bar. He wanted to smile at her. He wanted her to wave at him. He wanted to give her a hug. He wanted for them to do a shot of whisky. He wanted to maybe go home with her, maybe not, but at least make out with her uncomfortably and awkwardly on the sidewalk out front.

But then three weeks went by and Matthew never once saw Allison's pale, freckled face. He even came in on his day off once just to see if maybe she was coming in when he wasn't there. He still thought of Emma with every waking breath, but he was just upset that Allison – his distraction – wasn't there to distract him. It was like having a video game system with no controller. Tempting and worthless at the same time.

But it wasn't until after a full month since his night with Allison that things began to get a little strange for

Matthew. He had been feeling a little sickly on and off for a few days, but he didn't know exactly why. He put it off as stress and a possible cold he was fighting off and just went on with work and his life.

Of course, that all changed one lonely night when he was watching porn on his laptop. So, there's Matthew, watching one of his favorite porns on this fateful evening of his. What started as normal ended up as unusual when he found himself compelled to get to the end of the scene as fast as possible. Matthew actually found himself fast-forwarding just to get to the money shot – the point in the porn where the man ejaculates all over the girl's face and body.

"That lucky fucking bitch," Matthew found himself saying out loud as he watched one of his favorite porn starlets be doused with ejaculate.

Suddenly, this struck him as very odd. Matthew, at this point in his life, was in his mid-twenties and had never once entertained the idea of homosexuality. He wasn't against it or afraid of it, but he certainly knew that he was oriented toward women and not toward men.

So then why did he find himself jealous of women who were getting covered in semen?

Rather than analyze the situation, he went into the kitchen, took two shots of vodka, and promptly fell asleep. Matthew assumed he was just having a weird night, for whatever reason, and didn't feel the need to truly analyze the situation. And who can blame the guy?

Of course, a week later was when Matthew really started to wonder what the hell was wrong with him. That was when, rather than watch his normal porn, he found himself downloading the most depraved bukkake scenes he could find. Bukakke, for those who don't know, is a Japanese term for when multiple men simultaneously ejaculate on a woman's face. And we're not talking two or three guys, but a solid dozen or so. It's bizarre shit. Not really for those people we call 'sane.' But, oddly, he wasn't even masturbating to them. Instead, he was actually envious of them. Envious of the girls in the same way that one might be envious of a lottery winner. Matthew wanted to be that girl and he had no idea why.

Matthew, as he was rapidly discovering, had an unaccountable desire for semen. As much as he could find. For a straight male grappling with relationship problems, this was slightly troublesome and confusing.

For several days, work became hell for Matthew. Rather than look at the girls that came into the bar, all he could was check out the guys and wonder what their ejaculate was like. He was miserable. He thought nothing could possibly be worse than whatever he was going through.

Matthew eventually started talking to another bar regular named Evan. This guy, however, was much different from sweet, little Allison. For example, there are those that might have considered Evan gay. This was sort of unfair. Anyone who thought that Evan was gay probably also thought Burger King sold burgers. Which, unless you aren't following what I'm trying to say, meant that Evan was magnificently and grandiosely gay. Evan was so over the top, that a lot of gay men were actually offended by how gay he was. Like when a super slutty girl walks into a club and all the girls who forgot to wear underwear that night suddenly look at her and say "Damn, what slut." That was Evan.

So, Matthew and Evan were talking. Matthew was drunk. Probably too drunk. One thing led to another and Matthew told Evan about his current plight. This was because, at this sad point in his life, Matthew had two things on his mind – Emma and semen – and, much to his dismay, Emma was taking the back seat to the great, white custard.

Alright, I'm not gonna beat around the bush anymore. Matthew ended up going home with Evan. He swore to me on everything that is Holy that they didn't have sex. And, because of how fucking disturbing this story is, I believe him. But Matthew did suck Evan's dick. Twice.

"Twice?" I asked.

"Listen, you fucking halfwit..."

Matthew woke up in Evan's bed and was out of there faster than my senior prom date was the next morning after the big dance. But he did feel revitalized. Rejuvenated. His 'cold' was gone and his abnormal obsession with semen seemed to have waned, if not disappeared altogether. Not knowing what else to make of it, Matthew just assumed the whole scenario was some awkward, post-breakup shit he had never dealt with before and thought that now he could slowly rebuild his life.

Three weeks later, Matthew found himself in Evan's bed once again. And, like the last time, there wasn't any sex. Yet, Matthew couldn't keep himself from swallowing three rounds of Evan's manhood.

"I was suicidal," Matthew told me directly. "I mean, fuck. The girl I thought I'd spend the rest of my life with dumped me, I was stuck in a country I didn't really belong in, and I kept getting drunk and sucking some bloke's dick. How was I supposed to feel?"

"Fucked," I replied. "And not in the proper sense."

"Aye. Fucked without the fucking. Right grand."

Around this time, Matthew told me, he noticed some odd changes going on with him, physically. His lips, which had always been thin and extraordinarily uninteresting, were suddenly blossoming with an odd fullness. He hadn't really noticed it, at first, but Evan had made some comment after their second night together which made Matthew consult a mirror. He disturbingly found that Evan's comment about "cushiony lips" was horribly accurate.

"When in the hell did this happen?" Matthew asked himself while standing in Evan's bathroom.

The change in Matthew's mouth made him notice a few other bizarre changes that had happened over the last few months. Matthew told me, for example, how he lost his gag reflex at some point. This quite upsetting revelation came to him as he was eating an apple and, rather than coughing up a dislodged piece of green pulp, nearly died.

Thank god he had been at home and one of his roommates had rushed over to Heimlich maneuver him back to life. And if all that hadn't been odd enough, Matthew soon realized he had completely lost his taste for meat of any kind. It took over a week of a near vegetarian diet and a comment of the owner of Matthew's bar to make him notice how salads and falafels had become the staple of Matthew's diet.

It was about this time that Matthew began going online and checking out medical message boards about what could be wrong with him. At first, he said, most of his search results involved confused married men than anything else. Men that suddenly developed full lips were mostly classified as transgenders and a distaste for meat led, comically, to a series of militant lesbian sites. One night, in a fit of severe frustration, Matthew nearly destroyed his laptop when he tossed it across the living room. His roommate, who was watching TV in the same room, said that maybe they should go to the pub and have a drink. Matthew thought this idea sounded fantastic, but wanted a change of scenery.

"You know any good spots out of here? I want something different tonight," Matthew asked.

"I know just the place," his roommate said, who he only now mentioned was named Carl. They grabbed their coats and headed out the door.

The two headed into Greenpoint, an area Matthew had only been to twice before. Carl's plan had been simple – get drunk, mix with the regulars, cause a ruckus, go home. The ruckus was key. Make Matthew feel a little more relaxed and maybe let off some steam. Carl had no idea what Matthew had really been going through, but he certainly knew that some bad clouds had been brewing overhead.

Unfortunately, none of Matthew or Carl's plans panned out. After taking about seven steps into the bar, Matthew ran into Allison. She was sitting at the bar, looking as cute as ever, and sipping on what looked like a vodka and soda. Even though she was chatting up some other guy, Matthew had already imbibed a few other drinks at their apartment and was now a little tipsy. Or a little shiftaced. At this point in his story, Matthew was on his second gin on the rocks, his story was varying, and I was seriously wondering where the fuck Meagan was. Of course, I really had no choice in the matter and Matthew continued to carry on with little to no form of censorship.

"Hey, sweetie," Matthew said to Allison. "Where you been all my life? Or the last couple months, at least?" He thew a wink Allison's way.

"Oh, hey," she said and gave him a hug. "I've been around."

"Yeah? Around where? I used to see you in the bar all the time. Now you're like a bloody ghost. What happened to you?"

"I actually moved out of Williamsburg about a week after we hung out," she said. Matthew couldn't help but note her use of the term 'hung out' in relation to the night they spent together. He was less than thrilled. "I haven't really been back to the neighborhood since."

"Still, you could've..." Matthew began but stopped short.

"Could've what?" Allison asked.

"Nevermind. I was gonna say you could've called, but then I realized someone never gave me their number."

"Oh, yeah, guess I didn't," Allison said and suddenly began to look rather uncomfortable.

"Look, it's okay," Matthew said. "I get it. Really. It's no big deal. Gimme a hug, will ya?" She smiled nervously and the two embraced each other. "I'm gonna go have a few pints with my mate, kay? You be good."

"Okay," she whispered and the two parted ways.

Matthew admitted that he continued to glance at her from time to time during the course of the night, but he truly expected their encounter to end then and there. It wasn't until Matthew's distinct desire came over him and he began looking around the bar for the right man that thoughts and memories began creeping back into Matthew's mind.

"When was the first time I had the desire for semen? When did my physical changes start? Was it something that happened with Emma? Was it something that happened afterwards? Was it England? Was it America? Was it a person? Was it an event?"

Eventually, a light bulb went off in Matthew's head. Well, let's be honest, it was a really fucking drunk, flickering, cracked light bulb. I mean, drunk logic generally doesn't make any sense. I was once convinced that my ex-girlfriend ignoring my 3am booty call text messages actually meant she was just still in love with me and so she didn't want to see me because sleeping with me would just make her feelings for me too strong and confuse her. Right. That's drunk logic for you. And so Matthew's inebriated brain somehow put it together that all of his troubles came after the night he spent with Allison. So, it was clearly her fault. Clearly.

So, Matthew stomped back over to Allison and said, as firmly as a drunk man can, "We need to talk."

"O…okay," Allison said and put a coaster on top of her drink. The two found a shady area near the rear of the bar where the music wasn't so loud and stood facing each other. "What's wrong?" Allison said and was so awkward that nearby people who didn't know what was wrong could sense her discomfort.

There was a solid thirty seconds of silence while Matthew tried to formulate what he wanted to say to her. Matthew just swayed and rubbed his forehead for a long time while he tried to think. Eventually, he gave up. This was the best he could do:

"What the hell did you do to me?" he asked. Yeah, real fucking suave, right? Only one girl has blown the guy in three months and this is how he chooses to engage her. Smooth as fucking sandpaper.

"What are you talking about?" Allison said.

"There's something fucking wrong with me. I

don't' know what it is, but I know it all started after our night together. What, do you have herpes or something?"

Allison giggled at his ridiculous question.

"I'm not fucking kidding!" Matthew screamed out. He threw his drink on the floor shattering the glass on the cement ground. Allison and the surrounding patrons looked at him with shock. While he apologized to the strangers, he did not apologize to Allison.

"Shit, I knew four times would be too many," was all she said.

"Four times?" he asked, confused.

"I'm sorry, Matthew. I'm really, really sorry."

"About what?"

"The infection," she says calmly.

"The infection? You mean you gave me AIDS, you twat?! I…"

"No, just listen," she says and puts a hand to Matthew's face. He swats it away.

"Listen to what?"

"Just listen. And don't interrupt."

"I've had a bit too much to drink and I'm right pissed, but I'll try," Matthew says.

Allison takes a deep breath. Then, she ruins Matthew's life.

"So, I was infected about five years ago. Shhh, just listen. There had been this boy that I had had a crush on for a few years at the time. Unfortunately, back then he had a girlfriend that he was madly in love with. Anyway, blah blah blah, long story short, they eventually broke up. I made my move and we went out. We had this ridiculously passionate three month affair where he told me he loved me more than his ex and that he was so glad he finally found me and all that and so much more. I truly thought I'd found the man I'd be spending the rest of my life with.

"Unfortunately, he had somehow been seeing his ex while he was seeing me and, one super awesome day, decided to tell me how he was getting back together with her. Great fucking day in my life. I can't even tell you how miserable I was. You have no idea."

"I think I have some idea," Matthew interjected.

"Whatever. But, seriously, I felt like garbage. Not too long after he broke up with me, his best friend, Jeff, came online one day and asked how I was doing. He fed me all the appropriate lines and, well, it didn't help that he was cute, but he got me to come out with him and have a few drinks. One thing led to another and I went home with him, just like he was hoping I would. That night he found out that I had an oral fixation. Great for him. Shitty for me. Now, to the guy's credit, he did try to stop me from blowing him both the third and fourth time."

"Fucking shit," Matthew said. "You think you can try to make me feel a little less like a piece of shite?"

"Oh yeah, sorry. I'll try," she said.

"But so, yeah, sorry to rub it in, but I sucked that guy's dick a lot that night. Later, something…happened to me. I, I don't know, I just wanted to do it even more. But then…well, I guess you know what happened then."

"This is very odd moment in my life, Alli. Because while I understand how your story has a lot to do with what's going on with me, I'm entirely too pissed to put any of that shite together. Spell it out for me already."

Allison sighed and shook her head. "This is so unfair. I had to spend years trying to figure out what the hell was wrong with me. You have no idea how bad Jeff fucked me up and the years of therapy and bullshit I went through. Meanwhile, I'm gonna explain everything to you right in one, easy to understand package. Whatever. Here it is:

"You're a vampire, Matthew. Yeah, it's true. You're a living, breathing cartoon character. But you're different from most. See, vampires really have been around for tens of thousands of years. And what do you think happens in all that time? You think nothing changes? You think they're somehow exempt from evolution? From radiation? From genetic drift? No, they're a normal species like all the others. And, like all normal species, they change and mutate.

"Welcome to our lives, Matthew. We're mutant vampires. Drink that one in deep. A variation on a variation. A spin-off of a spin-off. What's weird about us, though, is that we don't need blood to survive. We changed somewhere along the line. Instead, we need well, you know what. Who knows what it is about blood that vampires need to survive – it's probably just some stupid protein or enzyme – but either way, we can't function without it. So, like vampires, our body's adapt to get what we need. But instead of fangs, we get fuller lips and the loss of gag reflex and all that. As for not liking meat, I just assume it has something to do with our body's inability to process protein and why we want cum. Just different protein, right? Just something our new biological systems are able to digest.

"So yeah. Semen vampires. You're one of them, Matthew. I'm sorry."

It's at this time that Matthew runs away from Allison and aims head-first for the nearest toilet. He doesn't even have time to lock the door before he barfs his brains out. To this day, he isn't sure if it was the liquor, the information, or the two combined that caused him to puke. Either way, Matthew claims the scene was horrific. When he finally returned from the bathroom, he found Allison back at the bar. He wiped his mouth and walked back over to her. He had one last question.

"So, does this happen to every guy you blow? I mean, you're hungry for cock. You clearly do this a lot. Aren't you worried about setting up an army of gay zombies or something?"

"Okay, Matthew, first of all, you're clearly drunk because…okay, whatever, I'm not gonna even bother."

"That's right you're not," he says, slurring his words, damn near unintelligibly.

"In case you're worried about all the guy's you've sucked off since you've developed your need for semen, asshole, no, it doesn't happen with every guy you're with.

Shit. Remember how I said four was too much? For some stupid, insane, reason, four is the magic number. You suck someone off four times in one night and they become a semen vampire. Why? Who fucking knows. This whole disease a stupid fucking joke to begin with. I've had it for years and you've only had it for months. So why don't you leave me the fuck alone and just get the fuck on with your life. It's clear you don't care about me and I don't care about you."

At some point during her tirade, Allison developed a noticeable amount of tears in her eyes. As soon as her rant was finished, she threw some money on the table and ran out the door. Matthew followed her, but it took him a few seconds to decide if he should and that was all the time she needed to disappear. Matthew said he's never seen her since. She disappeared forever.

The rest of Matthew's time at that Greenpoint bar was awkward, at best. He and his roommate, Carl, eventually left and never really spoke about what happened. Which, really was good for Carl, as he probably would've flipped out if he knew the guy crashing on his couch was a semen vampire. Luckily, that never happened. Instead, the two remained friends and Matthew eventually found his own apartment and moved out.

For the next year, Matthew continued on with his life. What else was he to do? He tried looking for support groups, but he found very little in the way of "I'm straight, but have an insatiable desire to swallow semen twice a day." Matthew began to live two lives, really. One life was his normal, day to day persona. The one everyone knew and loved and who he had been since the day he was born. His second persona was one that would go to the West Village on Friday nights at 3am and pick up men who were so fucked up on coke and ecstasy, they wouldn't remember who blew them the night before.

It was around this point in Matthew's life that the first of a series of fictional books came out. At first, the book called 'Twilight' held no real interest to Matthew. It was just one of another hundred, uninteresting pop culture books that were released each year.

Then, when fandom hit, Matthew read the back flap and opened the cover. He didn't really like what he found. Matthew found a fantastical, romantic tale about pretty, perfect vampires entangled in complicated and beautiful love affairs. But Matthew was a vampire who not only had been left by the love of his life, but also by the girl that made him what he was. Matthew was a vampire who didn't have love running toward him from all sides, but instead it fled from him as fast as it could. He saw it as a direct insult. For Matthew, it was like a firm kick to the genitals.

Define: rage.

In the middle of the Barnes and Noble at Union Square, Matthew threw a hardcover copy of Twilight across the room.

"Fuck you, Stephenie Meyer!" he screamed out as the book sailed across the hall. Patrons gazed at him with open mouths as they watched a display of board games and bookmarks tumble to the ground. "Who says vampires are all love and romance and horseshit, you fucking cunt?!" He yelled out to whoever was nearby.

Before security could escort him outside, Matthew voluntarily left. However, before he did, he walked up to one, particular security guard and screamed out, "Stephanie Meyer is a fucking hack who'll burn in hell!"

Needless to say, Matthew never returned to the Barnes and Noble at Union Square.

"This was all about two years ago," Matthew told me in the bar.

Meagan still hadn't surfaced and I was quite sure that she had gone home. Not only because she was a drunken mess, but because it was now after 3am and the bar was beginning to empty at a seriously accelerated rate. Matthew continued with his absurd and (I was beginning to think) fake story.

"You know what happened next?" he asked. *"Eight months ago Emma called."*

For some reason, that really brought me back to attention.

The love of his life, he explained, was reaching back out to him. It was like a beacon of hope. That something from his perfect past was stretching out to him, through time, to try and absolve his life and his ridiculous sins. This was it, he thought. This was when his whole life was change.

March fourteenth, he told me. March fourteenth of last year was the day he stood on the Brooklyn Bridge, looked down at the cold water, and actually put a leg over the rail.

"What stopped you?" I asked in far too casual a manner about why someone didn't commit suicide.

"Fear," was all Matthew said. "I'm a vampire, after all. Who says that fall would kill me? What if it left me alive and crippled for life? Not like I have a manual on how all this works."

I had no answer. But I did ask why he thought that seriously about suicide.

Matthew backtracked. He said that he thought long and hard about suicide on March fourteenth, but that Emma called him in mid-November. His long-life love had ended her relationship with the professor she had fallen for and realized the life she had before with Matthew was what she had always wanted. She called Matthew, spoke for nearly thirty minutes without interruption, claimed she didn't care if he was a street sweeper, and begged him for forgiveness.

He took her back without a moment's thought and told her that he could never stay angry at the love of his life. Matthew was so happy he cried in Emma's arms.

Unfortunately, like he said, this was in November. Matthew thought that he could beat his 'disease' if he tried hard enough. And to the fucker's credit, he did a good, goddamn job. It wasn't until March that he broke down.

March fourteenth may have been the day he considered suicide, but it was March twelfth that his fiancé walked in to find him sucking another man's dick in the comfort of their own bed. Long after Mr. Random left,

Matthew tried to explain. At first in lies. Eventually, he broke down and told her the truth. He told her everything that happened and said that he loved her so much his heart hurt but that there wasn't anything that could stop his disease.

Emma didn't believe him. She moved out the next day. That was March thirteenth. What happened the day after I've already explained.

"Today," Matthew told me, "is July ninth. Emma has moved and changed her phone number. She wants nothing to do with me. The love of my life and the greatest thing that's ever happened to me pretends I don't exist. The girl who made me what I am has disappeared into the sunset. I'm stuck with this life of sucking dick to survive, when all I want is a proper wife and family."

"So?" I asked to Matthew and the empty bar.

"So," he began. "How fucking important do you really think that random blow job from a strange girl really is?"

I stopped and considered Matthew's suggestion. Was he bullshitting? Had he made a strong fucking case? Or was he the cleverest homosexual alive who had distracted me until every interesting girl had left the bar and I was drunk and alone and had just fed me this very convincing story of how letting him blow me will help keep him alive?

Just then, an arm wrapped itself around my neck.

"Hey, sexy. Hope you haven't been lonely."

I turned and found Meagan had finally returned to join me at the bar. Wow. It'd only been a half hour.

"Where the hell have you been?" I asked.

"I just ran into some friends," she said. "Why? Don't be pissed."

At first, I was pissed. Then I wasn't. Then I looked at Matthew. He shrugged his shoulders and turned away and I thought of his entire, ridiculous story. Allison. Emma. Jeff. Carl. Semen. Everyone.

Oh, shut up. Yes, I was absolutely considering

Semen as a character in Matthew's story.

Point: I looked at Meagan and asked her one question. Luckily, in my drunken stupor, it sounded a lot more cute and humorous than it really was.

"Be honest, did you find some other guy on the way to the bathroom and blow him, too?"

Meagan hesitated. She looked me in the eyes and grabbed the back of my neck. "Maybe," she said. "But does that really make a difference about whether or not I suck your dick all night?"

I looked at Matthew again. He was still looking away from me. But his entire story rushed over me and all I could think about was love gained and love lost. That, essentially, Matthew lost the love of his life over a blow job. Over a single night of loneliness.

I took Meagan by the wrists and unwrapped her from my neck. She was hesitant, but also drunk. She gave way and asked what was wrong.

"Nothing," I said as I stood up and threw forty dollars down on the bar. "I just plan on growing old with someone I love."

Matthew, without turning his head, cracked a smile.

"Fine, you asshole. Like that couldn't have been me?" Meagan asked.

"Probably not," I said. "Just call it a hunch."

FUCK YOU, J.E. TOBAL

"Call me Jay."

"Okay, Jay. So, is there anywhere you'd like to begin?"

"I have absolutely no idea. I thought that was your job. I mean, I'm not trying to be a pain in the ass. I just….I mean, literally. I thought that was your job."

"It can be. Though sometimes I don't need to start the dialogue. Sometimes, you already know what you want to say. I always like to present that opportunity before I begin my own discourse."

At this point, I was already over it. I wish I could say I didn't obviously roll my eyes. Didn't shift my weight uncomfortably. Didn't exhale a deep breath and scratch my neck. But I did. Cause only thirty seconds into this farce, I already couldn't deal with the mind games.

"Frustrated?" she asked.

"No," I lied. "Maybe," I lied less. "I don't mind being here. Honestly, I don't. Just the less psychological warfare, the better. I'm more of a straightforward kind of guy."

"Okay, fair enough," she said and shrugged her shoulders. She adjusted her posture and looked at some notes in front of her. She sat in a large, comfortable, leather chair. Expensive. Worn. Beige. In front of her was a glass coffee table. It was empty save for a dozen random magazines. Men's Fashion. Women's Fashion. Sports. Children's Puzzles. Comics. Cars. Cruise Ships. The full thirty-one flavors of the human psyche on display for one to pick and choose at 'random'.

"So, you're a writer?" she asked. "What kind of writing?"

"Fiction," I replied. "A couple novels. Some short stories. Some non-fiction when the financial aspect of my life requires it."

"Must take a hell of an imagination to develop all those worlds and characters, Jay."

"Oh, stop. Flattery will get you everywhere." I feigned a blush and waved my hand in her direction.

She chuckled. "You're very comfortable around women, Jay. Is that unfair of me to say?"

"No, I feel like I've always had a good relationship with the fairer sex."

"Good. In light of why you're here, let's hear about that. Tell me about your relationship with women, Jay. What's it like, in general?"

"I mean..." I thought about her question.

"Jay?"

"Yeah?"

"You've been sitting there silent for about two minutes now. Just thought I'd make sure you were still with us on this side of reality."

"Two minutes? Really? I mean, I know I zoned out for a second, but really? Geez, I'm more tired than I thought I was."

"No worries. Let's just take a step back."

"Okay," I said and took a deep breath. I felt off. I noticed I had a tooth that hurt a little and did that bizarre, subconscious thing that all people do when they find a tooth that hurts and poke it and play with it until it feels like a lightning bolt ripping through their entire jaw. "How far are we stepping back? Like to when I lost my virginity?"

"I think that sounds like a perfect place to start."

"Okay, well, her name was Amber….."

* * * * *

When you're seventeen years old and a topless girl looks right into your eyes and beckons you towards her, you have no choice but to move your body in her direction. It's sorcery. Witchcraft. Mind-fuckery at its finest. The entire Mongol fucking horde could be behind her waving flaming swords at you and still, you'd look her right in the breasts and – so help you God – one foot would slowly move forward, one in front of the other. This sort of thing isn't an option. It's prehistoric programming. Primordial obsession.

This was how I met Amber. I was at a summer concert festival when I was walking by this tent filled with people. I stopped to see what the fuss was about. Turned out, the tent was the place where girls took their shirts off and got their naked chests airbrushed for free.

You could say I was really into this tent.

That's when Amber saw my scrawny, teenage ass and decided she wanted to see what truly awful sex was like. Cause out of a crowd of thousands of way better looking guys than me, she sought me out like I was some kind of a Greek God.

"Hey there," Amber said as she smiled at me from underneath the tent. She was only a foot or two away from me, behind a fold-up table. I smiled back and did my absolute best to not look at her mostly naked body. Of course, my absolute best meant I was staring directly at her mostly naked body. I'm a winner.

"Um, hi, I'm Jay…" I said in what I think was English. I offered my right hand as if to give her a hand shake.

Because smooth.

Instead, she gave me a hug. Oh, lord, what a hug it was. My knees almost buckled. My heart murmured. I'm pretty sure I pooped a little.

"I'm Amber," she said. Then, before I even knew what was happening, she brushed the side of my temple with her right hand. "I really love your eyes. They're why I beckoned you over."

"Yeah, my mom loves them, too," I said.

* * * * *

"So, it's safe to say you didn't always know how to talk to women," she said.

"Not. Even. Remotely," I replied and laughed. "I got better. Over the years. Very. Very. Slowly."

She chuckled. "Well, Jay, it's better to learn slowly than to not learn at all. Still, I'm guessing you eventually wooed this Amber?"

"Yeah, I didn't sleep with her that night, but about a week later. She had no idea I was a virgin. Well, maybe she did afterwards. Can't say I was very good in bed at the time. But we kept in touch after the festival and eventually it happened."

"And your relationship afterwards?"

"Well, it was hard. We were living in two different cities. I was enamored with the girl – I mean, she took my virginity and all – but she wasn't half as into me as I was into her. Eventually, it fell apart. Que cera," I said and shrugged my shoulders.

"And after that? Can you tell me more about some of your past relationships with women?"

"In what detail?" I asked.

"You tell me," she replied.

"I mean..." I began to say and leaned my head back. "I've ran the gamut. I've had long-term girlfriends. I've had one night stands. I've had girls who wouldn't leave my bed. I've had girls who kicked the shit out of me during sex..."

"Okay, hold on. That's an interesting one. You had a girl beat you up during sex?"

"Well...."

* * * * *

Isha was Afghani. Drop dead gorgeous. Except for the fact that she was born Afghani and thought the best way to dress herself was fully covered in loose fitting clothes from wrists to ankles. Meaning that if you saw this girl walking down the street, you'd have no idea how beautiful she was. Sure you could see her insanely dark, intoxicating eyes. Her comically full lips. Her sharp, sexy, jaw-line that led stealthily down her neck.

The first time I saw what was down her neck, I couldn't believe it. By then, her and I had already known each other for a few years. This was cause Isha had briefly dated a friend of mine a while back. But she was super private and so I never really got to know her beyond a few quick conversations.

That was, of course, until the two of them broke up.

Now, I wish I could say I was never one to fuck with my friend's exes. But well, that'd be a goddamn lie. I've fucked with lots of my friend's exes. Though I think they've probably fucked with mine, too. I'm not sure if that makes it okay? I don't know. This is weird.

Anyway, Isha texts me out of the blue one day and says we should get a drink. These are the first words out of her mouth when we meet up:

"This is John," she said, turning her phone around to me and showing me a picture of her boyfriend. "I really love him. He's been amazing."

"Well, I'm really happy for you," I said, honestly not giving a shit. This guy could've built her a castle filled with puppies or given her a jackhammer dildo machine and I swear, I wouldn't have cared either way. "So are we gonna get some shots or what?" I asked.

"Sure, I'm game for some fun!" she said.

Two hours later, she's on top of me. Naked. Naturally. And as she's riding me, I decide, as a man does, to make some mouth-to-nipple contact. That's when...well...

"Yeah, you like that, don't you? Baby's hungry for mommy's milk, aren't you?"

As she said these strange, bizarre words, I pulled myself away from her chest and looked up at her. Even though it was dark, I can only assume she saw the confused look on my face. And I say that I 'can only assume she saw my face' because the way she reacted was as though she did not.

Because as I looked into Isha's eyes, she lifted her right hand back as far as she could. It was almost as if she was reaching for something. Or stretching. Like there was something she was trying to get hold of that was barely out of her reach.

Then...

With full malice in her eyes, she slapped me across the face as hard as she could.

"What the fuck was that?!" I screamed as I held the side of my head, my ear ringing in agony.

"Oh, shut up," Isha said. "I know you boys like it rough."

* * * * *

"I don't mean to sound callous or insensitive when I say this, Jay, but it sounds like what happened last week isn't the first time you've had a violent, physical encounter with another woman."

"Okay," I said. "That's not fair. What happened with Isha and what happened at the bar were two very different things."

"How so?"

"Okay, well, for starters, what happened with Isha involved intercourse and what happened with Lisa involved...umm...sitting at a bar. And...not intercourse."

"Very structured language for a writer," she said, smiling.

"Shut up," I said and folded my arms.

"So, Lisa," she began. "Let's fold into that for a moment while we're on it. Do you know how that happened?"

"No," I said very stoically. "I swear to God. Or Buddha. Or Zeus. Or whoever. I'm not a violent person and never have been. I honestly have no idea what happened. As I'm sure you'd been told, I was very inebriated that night and was totally blacked out. And that's not some line to just get out of my horrible actions. I genuinely don't remember and I genuinely have no idea what transpired."

"Does that happen often?" she asked. "You not knowing what happened?"

"Not really," I said. "It happens occasionally. Maybe more often than I'd like, sure. But not often. More recently than it used to happen. Stupid old age."

"Does this mean it'd be safe to say you've been blacking out more often due to alcohol abuse than you used to?"

"Well, that's an extremely harsh way to put it. I don't think its alcohol abuse that's been blacking me out. I think its age. Honestly, almost one day to the next and I can barely hold my alcohol. I used to be able to drink almost a fifth of vodka without issue and now I drink three glasses of wine and don't know where I am. I've just been writing it off to getting older cause," and I shrugged my shoulders.

She chuckled. "Yes, getting older will do that to you. So, let's step back again for a moment then. What was your sex life before this so-called 'old age'?"

"Before old age…"

* * * * *

So, there's this website called Suicide Girls. Some people have heard of it. Some people haven't. Doesn't matter really. Nowadays, that old grey mare, she ain't what she used to be. But back in the day, boy, that website was something.

It's hard to explain, but imagine if someone smashed together Facebook with a Tattoo Magazine with OkCupid. Or, well, that's at least what it was like to me. A social networking extravaganza of gorgeous, tattooed girls who were all looking for a good time. Man, that website was a hoot.

This one party I went to, I met this girl named Richelle. Twenty years old. Tattooed and pierced. Body built for sin.

She immediately started flirting with me.

"I read palms, you know," she said as she turned my hand over. "This is your love line. Let's just say, it looks really long."

That's about when I turned her hand over and looked at her wedding ring. "Have anything you want to tell me?" I asked. "Cause your love line looks very distinct and, um, shiny."

We both laughed. "He and I have a great relationship," she said. "We trust each other. We would never do anything that would destroy our relationship."

"That so?" I asked.

"Yeah. Why you ask?" She smirked.

"Well, I saw you eying Jennifer over there. You know her and I have slept together before. It'd be really easy for the three of us to make a night of it."

"You should buy me a drink," she said. "Right now."

* * * * *

"Is it safe to assume that night ended exactly as I'm expecting it did?"

"It's very safe to assume that. It's also safe to assume that, even though she lived in a different state, her and I continued to have an extramarital affair for another two years."

"Something you're proud of?" she asked.

"Something that is just the way it is. You wanted to know about my sex life. I'm telling you about my sex life."

"Fair enough, Jay. And how about more recently. After this so-called old age?"

* * * * *

Brianna looked like the love child of a porn star and Alfred E Neuman. Which might seem confusing, so let me explain.

From the neck down, this girl was a 12 out of 10. Pick a curve and she had it. She even had curves where most people thought it was previously impossible to have curves. Her ankles were curved. It was genetically unfair.

Above her neck, things were different. She had really bad buck teeth, her ears stuck out, and even though she had really pale, blue eyes, her eyelids were on permanent vacation with the rest of her face. No matter her expression, she always looked incredibly stoned. Overall, her face looked like it might've once belonged to a Disney princess before a deer kicked it in with its hind legs.

Still, the whole package was pretty great. Brianna might not have been wife material, but she was still three or four-night stand material at the very least.

I met Brianna one night when I was out with two friends and she laid it on pretty thick. She walked up to me and introduced herself to me. Told me to come by the bar she worked at. Even gave me her number. So a few days go by and I go see her on one of the night's she told me she normally works. I'm not necessarily expecting to get laid, but I'm certainly expecting a warm welcome. Instead, I get…..

"Tonight's my last night, you know," she said to me as I walked up to her. She was behind the bar and it was the first time I'd seen her since I'd met her. It was a weird opening statement, but I went with it.

"Good, so we'll have plenty of time to go out this

week," I said and ordered a drink. I smiled at her casually.

"Not sure," she said as she handed me the weakest drink I've ever had. "We'll see."

"Well, what ab…" I didn't even finish my sentence before she walked away from me and started laughing with some other guy at the bar. I sat there and drank my drink for nearly a half hour without her ever making eye contact with me again. I just put ten dollars down on the bar and left.

* * * * *

"Even I find that a little extreme," she said.

"You find it a little extreme? Hell, I find it very extreme. I don't mind a girl rejecting me. It's a natural thing in life. But to have a girl throw herself at you only to reject you a handful of days later? Woof. You feel that one right in the jibblies."

"I can't argue that, Jay. That really must make you feel really, really awful."

"It's like you're both a psychic and a psychiatrist," I said.

"Okay, well, let's explore that. What happened, Jay? How did you get from being a kind of player to being rejected? Did anything happen in your life between those two periods?"

"Ah, great. It always comes down to her, doesn't it?"

"I'm sorry?" she asked.

"Joanna. It always comes down to Joanna."

* * * * *

I still have a hard time believing I met Joanna when I did. If ever an angel came down from heaven and saved a person, it was Joanna coming down to save my sorry ass.

I was in a bad place. I had lost my job. My grades in

school were plummeting. The relationship with my family was deteriorating into rotten monkey spunk. And cause I had no money, I couldn't even go out and get drunk with my friends and ease the pain. I just sat alone in my bedroom, night after night, and thought about the various ways I could kill myself without making it too much of a hassle for others to clean up.

Really, I was a very considerate suicidal maniac.

You're welcome.

One night I'm at this birthday party for a friend of mine. I had brought a six pack of the cheapest, shittiest beer on earth just so I could say I brought something. And while I'm drinking what could barely be considered fit for human consumption, Joanna sits down next to me.

"Ugh, you're drinking that? For real? Do you actually like that?"

"Fuck no. I'm broke as shit and this fermented farmboy ejaculate is the best I can afford. And whatever. Their steady diet of corn and date rape makes this beer taste moderately.......moderate."

Joanna laughed. "Well, if you could be drinking anything you wanted, what would it be?"

"Anything?" I asked.

"Anything."

"Come here," I said, and beckoned her close. "You ever heard of a Henny Hoo?"

"Huh?" she asked confused. "A what?"

"A Henny Hoo. Best drink ever made." Joanna looked at me questioningly. I leaned in closer and whispered in her ear, "It's a mixture of Hennessey cognac and YooHoo."

Joanna immediately pulled back and choked on her beer. "Shut up. That's either the funniest joke I've ever heard in my life or I'm so appalled in your taste in beverages it might be looping back onto itself into finding you attractive."

"So, what you're saying," I said. "Is that I win either way?"

"Oh, I can see it already. This is gonna end so horribly."

* * * * *

"And how long were you two together?" she asked.
"Almost two years."
"That's a long, solid relationship."
"That it is," I said.
"And so what ended it?"
"..........."
"Jay?" she asked.
".......I may have gone back to my former ways."

* * * * *

One of the most difficult things any man faces is looking the best sex he's ever had directly in the eyes and telling it to leave him alone. In my case, that sex was a girl named Alyssa.

Alyssa was this pocket-sized sex creature from the south. The Lord saw it fit to give her breasts larger than her head and morals smaller than her waist. Not to mention her ability to fellate. I mean, everyone knows blow jobs are great. Alyssa brought them to a whole new level. When you're clawing at the walls and screaming out the names of cartoon characters from your childhood, that's not a sexual experience nor a religious experience nor a psychological experience.

It's all three. And afterwards, our brains are so damaged from the experience, we walk around for three hours grunting like cavemen and being afraid of the telephone.

Men aren't smart.

Alyssa and I had drifted apart years prior to me meeting Joanna. I honestly thought I'd never see nor hear from the girl ever again. But then one day she sends me an online message very casually suggesting we meet for lunch and how she's so happy I have a girlfriend and how I'm in love. Twenty minutes into beer and chicken wings and I get one of these from Alyssa, ever the poet....

"I really miss the way your cock feels in my mouth."

The New York Times says that bar bathrooms are the number three most common places for sex in the five boroughs.

Or, at least, that's what I tell myself.

* * * * *

"So, how did it end?" she asked.
"The affair?" I replied.
"Yes. What came of the situation? I'm assuming Joanna found out."
"Yeah, I guess you could say that....."
"Jay?" she asked.
"Yeah?"
"You trailed off again and blanked out. I think we should look further into this...."
"Shit, yeah, I dunno. That doesn't sound good."
"Okay, well, before we end today's session, just please briefly tell me. How did things end between you and Joanna."

I shifted my weight in my chair. I picked at my teeth. I ran my fingers through my hair. I...

* * * * *

"You lied to me," Joanna whispered through tear-soaked eyes. "You said Alyssa was in your past. Was dead to you. How...why...do you not love me?"

I sat right next to Joanna and tried to hold her but she wouldn't let me. Every hand movement, every kind gesture, every nod of my head was regarded as an enemy action. Even my breath was seen as an cunning spy.

"Come on, think about it like this: You know how we always talk about our celebrity cheat list? The famous people we can fuck and it'd be okay? Well, just think of it like that. I just made someone on my list. It's actually amazing for me!"

I knew how downright stupid what I said was. Knew how awful and vitriol the words were. That I was trying to make light of a situation that was the least possible situation to make light of. I should've been prostrating myself before Joanna. Whipping my back with a rope tied with rusted nails. Kneeling on broken glass. Confessing all my wretched sins.

Instead I was making a joke about how what I did was awesome and how she should be proud of me.

Guess I can't say I'm surprised with what happened next.

Joanna didn't say anything; she just stood up and walked out of the bedroom. I sat there, staring at the floor, holding my head, and replaying in my head the dim-witted jokes I'd just been making at my destroyed girlfriend's expense.

The next thing I knew, Joanna was standing in the doorway of the bedroom. She was leaning against the doorframe, one hand in her jeans pocket and the other hand behind her back. Her head rested on the doorframe, too, and it made it look like she was just completely disappointed with me. Not angry or sad or anything that she should've felt. It was like she was thinking, "You little infant who shit himself and doesn't even know any better."

I don't know what was worse. Seeing her look at me like. Or knowing I deserved it.

That's when, out of nowhere, she showed me what she was hiding behind her back. This little pistol that her father had given her when she moved to New York City. He taught her how to use it in order to protect her from rapists, thieves, and let's be honest, from complete pieces of shit like me.

She pointed it right at me and smiled.

"Wh-w-wait, Joanna. Let's talk about th…" I stammered.

"Oh, stop it," Joanna said. "You're not worth it." Then she turned the gun to the side of her temple.

"Wait, stop!" I screamed and reached my arms out.

"Fuck you, J.E. Tobal," Joanna said.

* * * * *

Neither of us looked at each other for a while. She pretended to look at the papers in her lap. I pretended to not be a sociopath. All in all, I think we both failed. But the time and the stillness did make it easier for her to eventually break the silence.

"I…that's quite a revelation," she eventually whispered.

"Yeah, I know. Quite the bomb to drop. I like to ruin people's days like that."

"Not at all. I'm glad you're opening up to me so quickly, Jay. I hope in our next session you'll be just as willing to talk about these deep, personal matters. I sincerely hope we can find out what caused the altercation between you and Lisa last month. I sincerely think you want to find that out as well."

"Sure, doc. I'm all peaches and cream."

* * * * *

"I'm glad you decided to return to our sessions, Jay," she said.

"Right. You act like I had a choice," I said.

"You'd be surprised how many choose contempt of court and jail time over simple discussion."

"That's fair. I probably would be surprised by that number. I'd probably also be surprised at how human beings have IQs below 90. It doesn't mean I want to be associated with those people."

She laughed. "Fair enough. Do you think you're

smarter than the average person then? More together?"

"I'm no genius. But I'm also no idiot. I may not be head and shoulders above the rest, but I'm at least maybe a head above."

"Would it surprise you to learn that there's long been a link between above average intelligence and mental disorders such as depression, bipolarism, schizophrenia, and others?"

I thought for a minute. "Not really, I guess."

"Jay," she said. "I'm guessing you don't often check your text message record? Or call record?"

"No, why would I?"

"What about your email garbage folder? Or social media messaging?"

"No, of course not. Why on earth would I do any of that?"

"You may be interested to know that you and Brianna had talked a number of times via text message before you walked into her bar on the night you described her being totally disinterested in you."

"I'm sorry? That's completely untrue," I said and began to drift off.

"And I can only guess that the names Beth and Julie and Kyla ring a bell? These names also came up in your records. These girls also rejected you unexpectedly, yes?"

"No! I mean, yeah they did, but no! How would you know this? Who told you about this?!"

"No one told me this, Jay. Your phone records did. You gave me permission to check them. It was one of the papers you signed off on – an optional paper, I might add – when we began our sessions. I think there are lots of events going on in your life you are completely unaware of. For example, do you know who Joe is?"

I'm not sure why, but a shiver ran up my spine. It was involuntary. Like I sat on a giant block of ice. In the context of our conversation, the name just felt like a piece of electrified barbed wire that got shoved down my spinal cortex.

"No," I said. "I...Joe isn't anyone important."

"So, he's someone," she said.

"Yes...no...why does it matter?"

"Jay, you've been experiencing something for several months called 'lost time'. It's a psychological phenomenon that manifests most commonly when one is suffering from Dissociative Identity Disorder."

"...what does that mean?" I asked skeptically.

"It means, Jay, that these girls haven't just randomly been rejecting you and leaving you. It means you've had someone pushing them away from you."

"Are you saying..."

"Yes, Jay. That someone is you. You've been pushing them away. Or, not so much you, but a splinter of your personality. A version of yourself that's named itself 'Joe'. He mostly only manifests himself when..."

"When what? When some stupid bitch comes along telling me that I'm no good? Right, go fuck yourself! I don't have time for this bullshit! Go suck off a moose or something and leave me alone," he said and stood up. He made his way to the door and out of this psycho-babble bullshit house.

"Joe?"

"Yeah, what of it?" he replied.

"Since I have you here, I'd be very interested to know what happened with Lisa at the bar a few weeks ago."

"You mean that dumb girl I clocked in the face?"

"That'd be the one," she said.

"She was giving Jay lip. And for no reason. He was actually trying to be a pretty upstanding guy. A friend of his kept checking her out, but he was too shy to go over and say hi, so Jay did it for him. He even offered to buy her and her friend a round. But instead of saying thanks or no thanks, she just called him a pussy and said that he really liked her, but he didn't have the guts to say anything. She started calling him a creepy predator. That's when I shut her up."

"That wasn't very nice of her," she said.

"No, it wasn't," he said.

"I know you don't really want to listen to me or believe me, but I really would like it if you'd have a seat. I have some news about Joanna's death that may surprise you and...."

"What the fuck do you know about her?!" he screamed out.

"Oh, I know quite a lot about her. Presumably more than you do, Joe."

He ran at her. Fists high. Saliva flying out from between his teeth. Eyes bloodshot. Hair standing on end. "How dare you say such a…"

"Joanna isn't dead, Joe. Because she never existed."

Joe stood above her. Around her. Encompassed her. He breathed in oceanic breaths while baring his teeth and cracking his knuckles. He wanted to move in on her, but something in what she said made him stop.

"Jay," she said and looked up at us. "I know you're listening, so that's who I'm addressing right now. Please listen to me. You aren't Joe. Joe is someone who you've made...."

"SHUT UP!" he said.

"…up. In most cases of dissociative identity disorder, a traumatic event causes the individual to create a secondary personality to cope with the traumatic events that occurred within their life. In your case, you created Joe to cope with the loss and suicide of Joanna…"

"I did not!" we said.

"Her loss was insane and unbearable. She saved you from yourself and from a lifetime of misery. She was everything you wanted and needed and was perfect beyond measure," she paused and took a breath. "This was because you created her in your mind."

"I DID NO SUCH THING!" we said.

"I called her supposed parents. I called your parents. I called your friends. I called your siblings. I called the company you said she worked for. I called anyone who might've ever met Joanna Lansing. There is no record of the girl ever existing.

"Jay, you built the device you needed to survive. You built Joanna. A quirky, beautiful girl who understood all your odd behaviors and childish ways. But as perfect as you imagined her, even your own mind couldn't encompass your own infidelity. You were so ashamed at the affair you begun with Alyssa, that even your own psyche had no choice but to have Joanna – or, Joe, in female form – commit suicide. Unfortunately, this created Joe, the defiant male form that would go on protecting you from women who might hurt you."

I ran my hands through my hair. This was all too much to absorb. It's one thing to be told you're messed up, but it's quite another to be told your girlfriend of two years never existed. I started wondering about everyone. Friends. Family. Had I made them all up?

That's when I noticed her. Years had gone by. Decades really. But I'd never forgotten her face.

But there she was. Amber. That sweet, crazy, bowl of plum whackadoo pudding standing in the doorway of the office, arms folded, smirking at me. I gawked at her with wide eyes and tried to catch my breath.

"What?!" the doctor said. "What's going on? What is it you're seeing?"

"A-amber?" I asked. "What are you doing here? What's going on?"

"Fuck you, J.E. Tobal," Amber said and winked at me.

My eyes moved from Amber to the doctor. "I hope you like my company," I said. "Cause I think you're gonna be seeing me around for a long, long time."

A SINGLE SENTENCE:

BUDDHA THE DESTROYER

"And what is right resolve? Being resolved on renunciation, on freedom from ill will, and on harmlessness to life; but not on harm to material objects, for these things cause want and suffering and should be eliminated when attachments are formed: This is called right resolve."

- Sutta Pitaka, 400BC [on Right Resolve, the second element of the Eightfold Path (fourth of the Four Noble Truths)]

I.

Marcus Thomas woke up on a Thursday morning no different from any other. He showered, he dressed, he brushed his teeth. When he was finished, he went downstairs and sat down at the breakfast table. There, he was joined by his two younger sisters and his parents. Caroline Thomas, his mother, was just finishing scrambling a huge, pan full of eggs which she had already begun to portion out to Marcus, his sisters, and his father. Toast and juice followed shortly. As Marcus ate, he thought of Ellen.

Ellen was frequently on Marcus's mind as of late. She, a girl in his chemistry class, had caught his attention only three weeks earlier at the start of Marcus's junior year of high school. When Marcus got up in the morning, he thought of Ellen's smile. When he went to sleep at night, he thought of her green eyes. When Marcus was taking out the trash, he thought of Ellen's quirky remarks. And, late at night, Marcus thought....

Anyway, chemistry was Marcus's fourth period. This meant he had to sit through three, agonizingly boring classes before he would rush to Mrs. Adamson's chemistry class and sit down in his usual spot, just across the lab table from Ellen Parker. So, on this Thursday just like any other, Marcus sat in his third period class and was bored and thought of Ellen and waited.

Marcus, you see, was one of those confused, high school kids that didn't really identify themselves with any of the normal high school cliques. He didn't really care very much about sports, so the jocks and the preppy kids wouldn't have him. He had never tried any drugs before, so the stoner kids turned their back on him when he didn't know who The Grateful Dead were. Marcus enjoyed reading and watching the occasional science fiction movie, but not to the extent that he could discuss the intricacies of one film for hours on end. That meant the nerds didn't like him either.

No, Marcus Thomas was peerless; and not in any kind of grandiose, heroic sense, but in a more humble and unfortunate sense. He was a boy who was slightly uncomfortable with himself and his mouth full of braces and always thought that, if he was lucky, he could just sit off on the side lines and not be noticed. Marcus was content with just sitting across from Ellen Parker, glancing occasionally into her big, green eyes, and just exchanging the occasional passing remark. For an awkward 16-year old, it was all he needed and all he cared about.

So, as the bell rang at the end of this average and ordinary Thursday's third period, Marcus threw himself down the hallway at breakneck speed. He knew that after several weeks the other kids in his class would habitually sit in the same seats they were used to, but they weren't far enough in the year for that to happen yet. If Marcus didn't claim his seat, he could lose it to someone else. Marcus asked for so little. He didn't even want to imagine such a thing happening to him.

Unfortunately, when Marcus entered the classroom that morning, he found Jonathan Mack, the biggest nerd he'd ever met in his short life, sitting in his usual seat and with his nose buried deep in some high-fantasy novel. For a few seconds, Marcus only stared at Jonathan with wide, angry eyes. *You little fucking twerp,* Marcus thought. He seethed with anger. Marcus wasn't big, by any means, but Jonathan Mack was one of the smallest kids in his grade. Marcus briefly entertained the notion of walking up to Jonathan Mack, throwing his dorky book across the room, and telling him to get his nerdy, diseased ass off his lab stool.

Marcus, however, wasn't a complete social leper. Rather than make a fuss, Marcus sat down in a seat near his usual lab table and pulled out his text book. He began to look over the day's lesson as other kid's from his class filed into the room. Marcus ignored them and continued to learn the surprisingly complex workings of the surface tension of water as compared to other liquids.

Just then, no matter how much he tried to ignore it, Ellen drifted in to the classroom. She looked around, specifically at the lab desk she normally shared with Marcus and frowned when she saw Jonathan sitting in his place. Marcus saw this out of the corner of his eye and his heart leapt. Of course, when Ellen saw where Marcus had moved to and she waved at him, his heart started doing summersaults.

She. Ellen Parker. Waving at him. Marcus Thomas.

Ellen passed their usual table and sat down, as she had for the last three weeks, across from Marcus.

"Why you sitting over here today?" she asked him.

Marcus looked up at Ellen and was a complete loss for words. Yes, they had spoken on a few occasions over the last few weeks, but Marcus never imagined she had thought of it as anything special. Had they become something more without Marcus even realizing it? He tried to act calm. *What would I say if Ellen was just another friend?* he thought to himself.

"Huh? Oh, I walked in and Jonathan was sitting in my usual seat. Didn't really wanna sit next to him since he sort of weirds me out, right? Know what I mean?"

Ellen laughed. "Oh, I know. He's SO weird. I had him in History last year. You know he cried when he got a B on one of his papers? Geez, can you imagine? He's such a spazz."

"Oh, you don't even want to know what he did in English freshman year. I remember one time…"

"Wait, freshman year?" Ellen asked. "Wasn't he in the Gifted program? I mean, he never shuts up about it."

"Well, yeah. So was I. It's no big deal though. But listen, you gotta hear this," and as Marcus told his story, he couldn't help but notice Ellen's face brighten when she heard that he had been in the Gifted program, too. As Marcus spoke, he nervously stumbled the words of his story and blamed it on a lack of sleep. Ellen didn't seem to care, one way or the other.

Over the next month, Marcus and Ellen became closer friends. They began sitting with each other at lunch, often with no one else around, and talking on the phone a couple times each week. Marcus still didn't see Ellen completely as a friend, but what could he do? Friendship, he thought, was certainly better than nothing.

Ellen, Marcus began to discover, wasn't so different from himself. A lot of the boys, she said, were intimidated by her height of nearly six feet. This meant that she didn't have as many guys chasing her as Marcus would have thought. And, even though she was beautiful, she wasn't obsessed with her looks like a lot of the cheerleaders and the other preppy girls he knew. Ellen was sort of normal.

And, at one point, she revealed to Marcus that when she was in first grade, her cousin had had braces. She thought it was so cute back then and never really lost that childhood affection for braces. Marcus couldn't help but blush.

So, time goes by, and soon enough Marcus was tutoring Ellen in Chemistry. Marcus found the subject came to him as second nature while Ellen struggled with each and every concept. Marcus relished the fact that he could find yet another reason to spend time with her.

Then, one day, Marcus was at Ellen's house teaching her the finer points of stoichiometry. She sat at her dining room table as he stood over her, checking her work. Just then, she brushed her raven, black hair in front of his face. He couldn't help but close his eyes and breathe in the scent of her hair. Coconut. Pineapple. Mango. Everything tropical. He loved it.

"Please don't do that," he said, half-aware of what he was saying.

"Don't do what?" Ellen asked. She waved her hair along his cheek one more time. Marcus pressed his nose against the back of her head and simply swam.

Drunk off nothing but her proximity, Marcus made the boldest statement of his life. "Please don't get close to me like this. I'm so in love with you and I don't know what I'll do if you don't pull away from me soon."

"Sounds fun," Ellen said. She reached around and put her right hand on the back of Marcus's neck. She pulled him ever closer to her.

What happened next needs not be detailed. But high school is high school. The two became very close. Weeks went by where chemistry was sometimes tutored and sometimes ignored. Parents insisted they keep their bedroom doors open when they were together, but that still didn't prevent teenagers from doing what they do best. As much as any two people could be, Marcus and Ellen had fallen for each other. And, as all people do, young and old, secrets began to spill out of their mouths in hopes of trust and in hopes of comfort.

"I'm a...Buddhist," Ellen said one night as the two were lying in her bed, watching TV. She said the last word with shame.

"You are?" Marcus asked, surprised. "Like, a for real Buddhist? What about your parents?"

"Yes," she said, ashamed. "A for real Buddhist. My parents, too. We just try to keep it a secret from most people. Ellen tucked her head into her chest, worried of Marcus's reaction. "Do you hate me?"

"I could never hate you, angel," he said and kissed the back of her head. "I just don't understand. I thought Buddhists hated America. Aren't we against everything you believe? Don't you want us all to be miserable or something?"

"No!" Ellen said and turned around to face her boyfriend. "See, most people don't understand us. We don't hate America or anyone for that matter. We hate that people are attached to things. That they can't live without material possessions. Like, for example, what would happen if you went into Jonathan Mack's house and took all of his Dungeons & Dragons games and burned them or something?"

"Oh shit," Marcus replied and rolled his eyes. "Kid would probably lose his shit. After he screamed and freaked out for a good year, he'd probably cry like a spazz. It'd be sorta sad, actually."

"Okay, and what would happen if I took all your movies? Or books? Or video games?"

"Well, that wouldn't be very nice. I mean, I like my movies and books and all. I don't think I'd freak out like Jonathan, but I also don't think I see your point."

"Marcus Thomas," Ellen began, using his proper name as she only did when she wanted his full attention "You don't even understand. Let me try to help you. Don't you not like all the other groups of kids at school because they're obsessed with things?"

"Huh? What, no? Why would you say that?"

Without warning, Ellen sat up and straddled

Marcus's lap as he lay on his back. She put her hands on his shoulders as she leaned over him, staring him in the face. "What are the jock kids obsessed with?"

"Sports, I guess," Marcus said.

"And what are the druggy kids obsessed with...obviously?"

"Yeah, drugs...obviously."

"And Jonathan Tack and the so-called 'nerdy' kids?"

"I guess science fiction?" Marcus said, unsure. "And stuff like that? But what? I still don't get it."

"And what are you obsessed with, baby?"

Marcus had never really thought about the question. 'Obsessed' was a strong word. Not 'liked' or 'enjoyed' or 'wanted to do over and over again.' This meant 'what couldn't you live without.' Marcus had a long struggle trying to figure out what such a thing was. At the end, he could only come up with one answer.

"You," he said, at long last. Marcus then craned his head upward and kissed Ellen on the forehead.

"No, you big dork," she said as she laughed. "I'm not a material object. I don't count."

"Well, yeah. I didn't know that was one of the rules though. Believe it or not, I'm not a life-long Buddhist."

"Shut it," Ellen said and smirked at him. "Anything else?"

"Well, nothing then, I guess."

"See?! You're not that different from us at all. What, you thought it was just your braces I was attracted to?"

"I don't know," Marcus replied cautiously. "I still don't think I understand."

More time passed. Ellen and her parents showed Marcus what Buddhism was. He was shocked to discover that it was a release, not a trap. It also explained a lot of things about his life. For example, it explained how Ellen was just as much of a social outcast as Marcus was, but why she had been confident about it and how he had been squeamish. And also why Marcus cared more about his homework than his outward, physical appearance. And why he let things roll of his shoulders when everybody else he knew obsessed over the tiniest, littlest detail as though it were a life or death struggle.

In Marcus's teenage eyes, Buddhism explained everything.

Then, one night, while lying in the hammock in Marcus's backyard and staring at the stars, Ellen asks him a question.

"What do you think the world would be better without?"

Marcus thought for a bit. It was a complicated question, after all. There were so many things to find at fault with the world, how could he pick just one? It was a long time of swinging back and forth, swaying to and fro, before Marcus answered.

"Smart phones," Marcus said, at long last.

"Why?" Ellen asked, not in confrontation, but in curiosity.

"Being able to communicate wherever you are is great, don't get me wrong. But this whole immediate connection to everything? I mean, we both know kids at school who update online every ten minutes. 'In class now. Bored.' 'Still in class. God this sucks.' 'Haha. Someone just farted.' I mean, do we really need to know every stupid, fucking moment of everyone's day? And, oh, hey, send us a picture of the classroom while you're at it. Show us exactly how lame you are."

"Why?" Ellen asked again, trying to get to the root of Marcus's argument. "Why does that bother you so much more than anything else?"

"Because if you're so obsessed with letting people know you're alive, then you aren't really living. How can you ever experience anything if you spend all day staring at a screen and typing? Like remember when Rebecca Jacobs went to that wedding of her cousin's in Las Vegas? She spent all fucking day taking pictures, uploading them, typing messages, responding to other people's comments, and giving status updates. I mean, how the hell could she have actually had fun at that wedding? She was so concerned with letting other people know she was there and having fun, there's no possible way she could have done anything but look at her stupid phone the whole time. It completely destroys the human experience of being alive."

Ellen, taken with Marcus's speech, began to kiss him passionately in only the way that a girl taken with a boy can do. Ten minutes later, she finally released him from her grip. "Sorry," she said. "That really turned me on."

"That's me," Marcus said. "All sexy with my teenage angst."

Ellen giggled. "You know, it'd be even sexier if you followed through with those crazy thoughts of yours.

"Huh? You want me to stop people from using their phones?"

"Nooooooo. But if the phone's didn't exist...." Ellen wanted Marcus to put the last piece together.

"You want me to turn back time and stop smart phones from being invented? Look, I'll try, but I make no promises."

"An act," Ellen said. "All it takes is an act."

"What the hell are you talking about?" Marcus asked.

Over the next few weeks, Ellen explained to Marcus how an act can be a symbol. How only one or two can affect great change. She told him how Rosa Parks sat down on a bus and started a change for minorities in America. She explained how a few planes bombing a Hawaiian island eventually led to two nuclear bombs being dropped on the island of Japan; a rift in social and political ties which would never be recovered. She detailed how a man named Rodney King was beaten which made the whole nation open a blind eye to a wretched situation in their own country. Then she reached into the past and talked about how a handful of photographs by a man named Jacob Riis made the entire upper class of late 19th century New York City realize how half their population was living in unprecedented squalor.

An act, she explained, if powerful enough, can do so much more than he could ever imagine. Marcus Thomas absorbed this idea over several months and eventually took it to heart.

Then, midway through his senior year, Marcus performed the most righteous and just act of his entire life. Using gasoline from his parents' car and a few other trinkets he picked up at the local mall, Marcus Thomas made a small, but powerful, bomb. He placed this weapon in the largest cell phone store of his town and detonated it. The explosion happened around 4am of, not surprisingly, an ordinary Thursday morning.

Marcus had created a long-range detonator (with the use of a cell phone, ironically) and didn't know the extent of the damage until the next day. It was at the breakfast table with his parents and sisters when he saw the devastation on the morning news. The building, while not leveled, was ravaged enough that it needed to be bulldozed and rebuilt from scratch. Marcus tried to hide his excitement, but he was sure his parents saw the smile creep in the corners of his mouth whenever they started to turn their head.

Then, a knock at the door. Marcus's father, James, answered the doorbell to find two police officers asking if his son was at home. Marcus could hear this conversation from the dining room and panicked. He ran to his room, without warning, and began to find every bomb design and detonator sketch in his room and put them in his trash can. He was seconds away from lighting the garbage on fire when the two policeman entered his room. Without even hesitating, one policeman tackled Marcus while the other went for the garbage can.

During Marcus's trial, Ellen never once showed her face. Marcus understood why, but he was still crushed. His love, the girl that showed him the way, wouldn't even stand by his side as he was judged and sentenced. And what a sentence it was, since Marcus had turned eighteen only two months earlier.

After all, Buddhist terrorism was the highest capital crime. It had been since after the first World War when the first Buddhist terrorist attack took place on American soil. Nothing was more of a threat to a democratic, capitalist society than a Buddhist extremist.

Marcus Thomas, still a senior in high school, was now an imprisoned enemy of the state.

II.

Kirsten Parker, Ellen's mother, saw the look on her daughter's face as she watched the morning news. Kirsten didn't know how, but she knew that Ellen was somehow involved with the bombing that was being reported. She looked at her beautiful and, she thought, innocent daughter and wondered where she went wrong.

Kirsten, you see, had converted to Buddhism when she was twenty-one. She was in college taking a class on comparative sociology when she met her TA, Jared, and was awed. Jared had studied Buddhism to the point that he had secretly converted when he was in Asia doing field work for his masters degree. He had such a passion for this radically divergent, yet misunderstood, religion, that he convinced his favorite student not only to convert herself, but eventually to marry him.

After they both graduated, Kirsten and Jared spent many a happy year living as Buddhists in a suburb just outside of Chicago. While most neighbors and random acquaintances didn't know their secret, all of their good friends knew where their beliefs lay. These close friends and trusted colleagues understood the difference between a practitioner of religion and a fanatic. Kirsten and Jared only maintained their secrecy because they didn't believe the public at large would feel the same way as those that knew them personally.

Though, as Kirsten Parker sat and watched the news on a not so ordinary Thursday morning, she couldn't help but wonder if she had made a few wrong decisions in Ellen's upbringing.

"Ellen," Kirsten began, choking back the tears in her eyes. "Can you believe what happened? Who would do such a thing?"

"I dunno. I guess someone brave enough to stand up for what they believe in. I think it's pretty hot. I wouldn't mind knowing the guy who did that."

Ellen's half-confession was clear enough for Kirsten. She got up from the kitchen table, picked up the phone, and dialed Marcus's mother, Caroline. It didn't take more than a handful of sentences to confirm the horrible truth that Kirsten was dreading.

Ellen had turned her boyfriend into a terrorist.

"You're staying home from school today," Kirsten said as she walked back into the kitchen, phone still in hand. She turned it on again to call her husband and let him know that he needed to come home from work for the day. Jared understood all too well and was in his car before he had even hung up his cell phone.

While Kirsten sat in her room and waited for her husband to get home, Ellen sat in the living room and watched the news. The young girl tried calling Marcus, but his mother had answered instead and promptly hung up the phone. Ellen continued to try and talk to her love, but Marcus's mother would allow no such thing.

Ellen didn't care. She was ecstatic. Marcus was everything she thought he would be and more. Ellen sat cross-legged on the couch, filled with fire, and imagined herself in the courtroom, behind the bench, supporting the man she loved.

Finally, Jared got home. He saw his daughter sitting in the living room, but didn't have the strength to look at her just yet. He scrambled upstairs to his bedroom where he found his wife sitting on the floor, looking at old family photographs.

Soon enough, Kirsten was crying and Jared was screaming and the two tried to figure out what they could have done differently, if anything. Had they talked to Marcus about Buddhism over the last year? Absolutely. But had they said anything about blowing things up or about this radical eradication of objects? Absolutely not. Kirsten and Jared knew what Right Resolve meant, but they interpreted it much differently from the terrorists. It meant a lack of attachment yes, but not an outright destruction of private property. How, then, did their daughter not agree with their version of Right Resolve?

"It's this crap media," Jared said at long last. "We're too far removed from other Buddhists. Ellen has nothing to base her faith on but us and the fucking television. And, let's be honest, the television is a lot more convincing than mom and dad to any teenage girl."

"Well, what are we supposed to do?" Kirsten asked. "Not let Ellen watch television? Or not let Ellen date? For Christ's sake, Jared, she loves him. You've said so yourself. How do we know she won't do this to another boy? Or four other boys? Honey, this is Marcus. Poor, sweet Marcus and he's now facing criminal charges. What exactly do we do?"

Jared paced around the bedroom several times without saying a word. Finally, after ruffling his dark, curly hair and undoing his tie, he sat on the bed next to his wife and deflated.

"I don't know," he said, at long last. "I feel like I've spent my life trying to understand people and now I can't even understand my own flesh and blood. I...I don't know..."

"No, sweetie," Kirsten began. She put an arm around her husband and rubbed his neck. "Don't put it all on yourself. It's like what you said: Ellen has nothing to understand of her religion but what we tell her and what the media tells her. We're only two people. To her, the television is the rest of the world. What competition is that?"

"Well, yeah, but it's like what you said before: What can we do? Stop her from watching television?" Jared asked. Frustrated, he buried his face in his hands.

"No," Kirsten began. "But what if Ellen knew more Buddhists who weren't extremists? More Buddhists her age?"

Jared pulled his hands out of his face and looked at his wife with more than a little bit of skepticism. "How do you mean?"

"Well," she began and paused. She could tell that Jared already knew what she was about to say. She said it anyway. "What if we moved to a city where there were a lot of Buddhists? Like New York?"

Jared Parker had heard the suggestion of moving to New York City over a dozen times and was outright sick of it. He loved Chicago. It was where he was born, where he was raised, where he went to college, and where he met the love of his life. He couldn't imagine what force on earth could get him to move away from such a perfect city.

And it's just at that point in life, when someone swears they'll never ever do something, that fortune chooses to prove them wrong.

"We're not moving to New York," Jared said, reflexively. "So help me."

"Have you really thought about this, Jared? I mean, really?" Kirsten pleaded. "I know how much you love Chicago. I really do. But think of our daughter. She's dying here. Go, look at her. She turned her boyfriend into a terrorist. I heard her talking to the goddamn television. You know she's even proud of what she's done? That she supports what Marcus did? Hell, that she inspired him? Tell me, please. Tell me, what do we do with our daughter? Please, tell me, Jared."

As Kirsten wept, Jared stared at the floor, motionless, for a long period of time. He didn't know what to say, or if any words could be said at all. He simply fidgeted with the corner of his shirt and thought, as though some other solution would simply throw itself at him.

"Ellen needs to be surrounded by her peers," Kirsten continued. "Not just by adults that are Buddhists, but by teenagers that are Buddhists. That way she can see and understand that we aren't all extremists. Shit, Jared, do you realize that, by media standards, she probably thinks we're the weird ones?"

Jared still had nothing to say. He knew his wife was right. But still, he found it hard to concede.

"Isn't there somewhere closer than New York that Ellen can be among peers?" he asked.

Kirsten hugged her husband and gave him a sweet kiss upon his cheek. Then, she spoke.

"Pumpkin," she began. "Please, give me suggestions. I don't want to be right here, I really don't. But if you can think of a better solution, please tell it to me. Please, tell me there's something easier we can do. If any time I can be wrong it my life, I want it to be now. I want to be wrong. Please, please, please, prove me wrong."

Jared sat and thought and thought and thought and still came up with nothing. He told his wife he would think of a solution in a few days, but after two weeks, he still had no new ideas. And, at long last, Jared Parker conceded to his wife's proposition of moving far from the home he loved to a city he only remotely understood. In his daughter, Jared found the force that would make him do the thing he swore he would never do.

So, as the first days of Marcus Thomas's trial began, Kirsten and Jared sat at home packing their possessions. Ellen reluctantly tossed her clothes and trinkets into boxes, but would be no part of the move, overall. She was both furious and devastated that her parents had not only decided to move, but forbade her from being involved with the criminal trial of her boyfriend.

But, before Ellen could act out, the Parker family was gone. Upon moving to Brooklyn, Jared and Kirsten changed their last name to Johnson and Ellen had no choice but to do the same. Ellen tried to act out a number of times, but the drastic societal change wouldn't have it. Ellen pushed her boundaries and her boundaries pushed back.

Before they knew it, Ellen was changing. Kirsten and Jared could only hope that it was for the best.

III.

Ten years later, Ellen was standing on the stage of a college auditorium and facing a mostly bored audience. She was speaking, as she had done countless times before, to a college-aged audience on the proper practices of Buddhist behavior.

"Don't listen to what the media tells you," she said. "Buddhism isn't about terrorism. Not all of us believe in the destruction of private property."

Despite the unreasonably attractive woman than Ellen had become, most of her audience ignored her. The men in the audience could tell she was good-looking, but they were uninterested in her words and were easily distracted by the younger girls with less to say and more to show. And, conversely, most younger women hated her because she wasn't only beautiful, but intelligent and outspoken as well.

Ellen Parker-Johnson didn't care what they thought. You see, in Ellen's lifetime, Buddhist terrorism had increased dramatically. In the 1980's, there was an average of three terrorist attacks per year. In the 1990's, this increased to a half dozen or more. By the 2000's, it was a terrorist attack just about every month. People everywhere lived in a bizarre sort of fear. Buddhists, of course, would never take a human life. This was against everything they believed. But every time a new cell phone, game system, special edition DVD box-set, or random gadget was to be released, warehouses and stores would go up one night in a ball of orange fire and black smoke. No one feared for their lives, but they feared for anger, for destruction, and for the occasional unplanned injury.

This is exactly what Ellen Parker-Johnson was preaching against in this very college auditorium. She condoned the behavior of terrorists with every breath she took, but she also condoned the extreme desire that most people had toward the very objects that were being destroyed.

"Love your parents," she said. "Become attached to them without question. Feel that way about your friends. About your boyfriends and girlfriends. About your relatives. About strangers you meet on the street. Please," Ellen pleaded. "Become attached to humans. Just don't become attached to objects. That life will lead you to nothing but misery."

Ellen knew, unfortunately, that she was preaching to deaf ears. She watched as each pair of young, confused eyes, drifted away from her attention and toward the attention of the electronics in their hands. The students took pictures of her and of the other students. They sent text messages to each other. They updated their online, social networks. And, for a brief, fleeting moment, Ellen remembered a conversation she once had with a boy in a hammock and shook her head in despair.

Two weeks later, Ellen was in front of her normal audience. She wore a beautiful, aqua-colored dress that accentuated her figure and features more than most men or women were comfortable with. Ellen liked this level of discomfort. It allowed her to approach people disarmed and open to suggestion. So, when she asked them for donations to her charitable foundation, Buddhism for America, they were only more than happy to give.

Ellen spoke passionately, for thirty, beautiful minutes as an audience of nearly two thousand people listened to her eloquent words. Then, when her captive audience thought the evening was at its end, Ellen raised her arms. With them, a crimson curtain drifted from floor to ceiling.

The audience gasped as they saw a beautiful, colorful, and intricately designed Tibetan mandala before them. Four Buddhist monks in traditional robes crouched carefully above the mandala and poured multi-colored sand carefully into the bizarre design. And, in order to make the spectacle more visible, a camera was positioned above the mandala to project the scene upright onto the rear wall. Ellen proudly displayed this scene as the mandala neared completion.

"Buddhism," Ellen began. "Is about impermanence. Nothing is forever. To believe so is to cause yourself pain."

As she spoke, the Buddhist monks finished their work and humbly backed away from their design. Their end result was nothing short of breath-taking. Flashes went off as photographers and spectators alike captured images of the painstakingly designed mandala. It was beyond beauty and beyond expectations. No one in the audience had ever seen anything so spectacular in their lives.

It was then, as flashes were still going off, that Ellen clapped her hands and said "It's time," that the Buddhist monks got back down on their hands and knees and began to smear the mandala they spent days perfecting. Crawling slowly from edge to edge, they mixed every color and line long passed the point of retrieval. Gasps echoed throughout the room.

"This is what you need to understand," Ellen said into the microphone as the mandala was destroyed forever. "True Buddhism isn't about random terrorism or senseless destruction. It's about the understanding that all things are fleeting. The idea that material objects won't last forever, so you shouldn't be attached to them; that you should destroy them rather than love them. This is what Right Resolve means, not what the extremists would have you believe."

"I love you, I love everyone, and I even love the

amazing technology that man creates," Ellen said. "But I can live without it and I that hope you can to."

Just at that moment, a minor explosion occurred at the rear of the auditorium's stage. As people panicked and hurled themselves toward the exits, Ellen and the monks were thrown across the stage into the front rows of the audience. No one present at the explosion sustained any serious injuries, but the damage done to the auditorium was significant. For a short time, no one was quite sure if the what happened was accidental or on purpose. Whispered rumors filled both auditorium hallways and hospital corridors.

Six hours later, a statement was released to the media. Responsibility for the explosion was claimed by a group known famously as Soka Gakkai. This infamous group cited the reason for the bombing as a true destruction of objects – not only complete and total eradication of the mandala, but of the auditorium that held it as well.

Of course, what truly surprised Ellen was the fax that she received later that afternoon, while she was still in the hospital. It appeared that the leader of Soka Gakkai, a man who's identity had remained a mystery for years, had requested the audience of Ellen Parker-Johnson at his private home in Japan. He had already bought her a first class plane ticket and detailed expressly how he would find a refusal to his invitation extremely insulting. Ellen was taken aback.

And as if this wasn't all surprising enough, the fax was signed by a name that Ellen found familiar. It wasn't a Japanese name, but an American name scrawled across the bottom of the page in blue ink. After ten years apart, it seemed that Marcus Thomas still had a way of getting Ellen's complete attention.

IV.

The apartment that Ellen entered was much more modern and clean than she had expected. You see, Sokka Gakkai was a radical Buddhist terrorist organization responsible for roughly one-third of all terrorist attacks on American soil. According to US intelligence, members of the group were extremely difficult to track down because they had chosen to live in the remote mountains of the nation's northern islands. Even assistance from the Japanese government provided little help, at best, in locating the extremists

So when Ellen landed in Tokyo and went on a short, twenty minute car ride to a beautifully modern apartment building, she thought there must have been some mistake.

Marcus explained to her that no, there was no mistake.

"We're actually extremely easy to track down," Marcus said. "Do you know that we're registered with the Chamber of Commerce here?"

"What?" Ellen asked. Her eyes were wide and her forehead was wrinkled. "How does that make any sense?"

Marcus handed her a cup of green tea and invited her to sit down. As Ellen perched herself on a large, white ottoman, she turned her gaze to the huge, floor-to-ceiling windows that comprised the entire west wall of the fifteenth-story apartment building. Outside, life was hectic. She watched cars zip down the road and bicyclists scurry close to the sidewalk. In the near distance, skyscrapers hemmed in the view. Ellen thought they made the world seem somehow both massive and closed in at the same time.

All of this was in stark contrast to the apartment itself. Everything inside spoke of modernity and serenity. For example, most of the furnishings were white – white leather couch, white fur rug, white marble floors, white polished walls, even a white teacup sat comfortably in Ellen's hand.

Marcus wore all white, too, but the outfit seemed more fitting of a man in 1960's Cuba than it did of modern Japan. And Ellen also noticed that other things had changed with Marcus aside from his attire. For one, he had grown his hair out long enough that it could just barely be put behind his ears. He also stood only around five feet and eight inches high (not growing even a centimeter, as many men do, after high school), but worked out enough that his body appeared to be in immaculate condition. Marcus was also barefoot and Ellen could make out just the slightest bit of a tattoo that poked itself down from his calf and onto his foot.

"The American government doesn't want to catch us," Marcus said.

"Hmmm?" Ellen said, her consciousness being shifted back into their conversation.

"You with me, angel?" Marcus said as he snapped his fingers in her direction. Even though she was agitated by it, Ellen couldn't help but blush at the old nickname.

"Yes, I'm with you." She took a sip of her green tea.

" Do you know the total cost of damage my group incurred on American products last year alone?"

"No," Ellen answered immediately. "Nor do I really care to."

"A half billion, give or take," Marcus replied calmly.

"Why are you proud of that?" The question had a sour note to it.

"Who says I am?"

"It's practically the first thing you told me. And I wasn't even curious. Why tell me at all if it didn't fill you with some sense of pride?"

Marcus took a sip of his tea and looked up at the ceiling in thought. He took a deep breath and let it out slowly. Ellen watched as a brightly colored bird flew outside the wall of windows.

"Okay, let me ask a more direct question," Marcus said, at last. "What do you think the loss of a half billion dollars of goods does to the American economy?"

Ellen didn't fully understand the question. While her personality had many strong points, she was also always the first person to acknowledge her weak ones. Of those weak points, economic theory was uncomfortably close to the top.

"I really have no idea," Ellen said, trying to sound confident.

"Interestingly, it affects the economy positively," Marcus began and stood up. He walked over to face the floor-to-ceiling windows as he continued speaking. "See, it's really just simple supply and demand. The less of something there is, the more expensive it is. The more expensive it is, the more money is being pumped into the economy. The higher flow of money means more taxes, more jobs, more of everything. Every time I destroy something, the American economy gets better. And, when the American economy gets better, so does the Japanese economy."

"Well, now I see where you get the nice apartment from," Ellen said. "Any other perks you get from being a terrorist."

"You have no idea." Marcus craned his neck around to look at Ellen. She looked back at him as though he were a demon. He winked at her once and turned back toward the glass.

Just then, the largest Japenese man Ellen had ever seen in her life entered the sitting room from an adjacent hallway. Both his face and his head were shaved clean apart from a small patch of hair at the bottom of the man's chin. He wore an expertly tailored and pressed suit accented only by gold rings on both of his thumbs. As the man approached Ellen and placed a manilla file on the table before her, Ellen had an epiphany. She looked toward Marcus.

"You know, you all may be the least Buddhist

group of people I've ever seen in my entire life. This apartment, your attire, this goon's attire, the car I arrived in. I've never seen a deeper love of physical objects. How are you extremists, much less Buddhists?"

"Fuck Buddhism," Marcus said simply. "Open the file."

Ellen was floored at Marcus's comment. In a daze, she turned toward the file filled with papers and accidentally dropped her teacup. She had forgotten it was even in her hands.

"Don't worry about it," Marcus said without turning around. "As you'd say, it's all just 'things'."

Ellen picked up the file and rifled through the loose papers. In her hands was a collection of everything from newspaper clippings to internet printouts to independent statistical analyses to (what appeared to be) declassified government documents. None of it made any sense to her.

"Marcus, what the hell am I looking at? It looks like, if I even understand half of what's going on, that the US government advocates terrorism."

"I always knew you were a smart girl." Marcus smiled and Ellen could see the reflection in the neatly polished glass. "But we had also sort of already established that, no? The US government could find me any of day of the week, if it really wanted to. But considering I'm actually helping them out by blowing shit up, why the hell would they want to?

"So, take it a step further," Marcus continued. "What happened in August, 1936?"

"The first Buddhist terrorist attack," Ellen said, a knee-jerk reaction. "Anyone who's taken American history knows that. The destruction of the Chrysler Building in New York. Why?"

"Look through your papers. Find out for yourself."

Ellen began sifting through the file, trying to ignore anything recent and focusing only on articles referring to 1950 or earlier. After thirty minutes of reading, re-reading, comprehending and second-guessing, she refused to believe the conclusion that Marcus was trying to force on her.

"The US government did not invent terrorism, you asshole."

"Says who," Marcus asked, leaving his view of concrete and steel. He sat back down on the couch and stretched out, putting his feet up on the coffee table. "Says you? Psshhh, bad reference."

"Fuck you, Marcus. Seriously, fuck you. I've made this my entire life. How dare you belittle it." Ellen threw down the file, but the papers merely smeared outward a few inches. "Did you really fly me here just to tell me how dumb I am?"

"God, after all these years, I still can't believe how sexy you are when you're angry." He winked at her and blew her a kiss.

Ellen sneered at Marcus and wondered how the boy she loved grew into this man that she feared. As she turned away from his face, her eyes couldn't help but graze past the manilla file filled with old papers still resting on the floor. She asked a question.

"Since I don't imagine you're putting me back on a returning flight to the States until you're done with me, what the fuck on earth makes you believe that the US government invented terrorism? Other than the half-cocked theories in this file."

Marcus put his hands behind his head and relaxed. "I will openly admit, as anyone should, that the attack on the Chrysler Building was the result of a handful of insane Buddhists with more than a little hatred toward American decadence."

"Thank you," Ellen said, bowing her head ever so slightly to the right.

"You're welcome," Marcus replied. "Of course, those infamous Buddhists numbered all of seven and were executed, secretly, by the US government within one week of the attack."

"So then why did all those other attacks occur throughout World War II? And up until today? Some gingerbread men and elves were blowing up buildings out there until you came along?" Ellen asked, curious and angry.

"No, but a Great Depression needs a Great Revival. The US government couldn't have seen another World War on the horizon. They needed something immediate to pick up their economy."

"Back to the supply and demand story then? Too bad that didn't make sense back th..."

"No shit it didn't make sense back then," Marcus interrupted. "But war does make sense. You know how many jobs a war effort creates? How many jobs 'national defense' provides to this day in the U.S.? An unseen terrorist was the cause not only for a national paranioa, but a cause to return to basic values, basic government, a massive increase in the job market, and a very simple international policy. It gave a confused nation order."

"Bullshit," was all Ellen could reply with.

"Bullshit? Bullshit?!" Marcus stood up from the white couch. "How? How can you think this is all bullshit? You're holding the proof in your own hands! Or, you were until you threw it on the ground."

"It's bullshit because I've met the Buddhist terrorists myself!" Ellen shouted. "They aren't secret government agents. They're true Buddhists, from East Asia, that believe in the destruction of objects to prevent attachment. I've met these people firsthand, Marcus. Have you?"

"Oh, how far the prodigal son has fallen," Marcus said and looked down at Ellen with a unique sort of sadness. Ellen couldn't place it. The huge Japanese man in the pressed suit could. It was the same look he saw his little boy give to his grandfather when the old man couldn't remember the child's birthday. It was half raging-disappointment and half utter-confusion. The Japanese man remained silent. Marcus did not. "You really don't understand, do you?"

Ellen stood up, blood racing through her veins, with the intent of screaming at Marcus until she passed out from exhaustion. She opened her mouth and right as she began to shout, he grabbed her by the shoulders and forced her back down onto the ottoman.

Marcus bellowed. "When you were a little, fucking teenage girl, Ellen, please, for the love of fucking God, please let me know what devout terrorists you were personally introduced to you." Strands of saliva flew from Marcus's mouth as he screamed. His face was purple with anger. Ellen cowered with fear. "Oh, no, that's right. You didn't know any. It was the television alone that convinced you that blowing shit up was the totally awesome Buddhist thing to do. Terrorists created by nothing but media attention. Factions created news stories that didn't get caught and kept recruiting and training. Fucking funny how that works, isn't it? Ha goddamn ha."

Ellen slipped off the ottoman and onto the floor. She turned her head to stare out the floor-to-ceiling windows, but found no visions of comfort. Tears streamed from her eyes. The distant skyscrapers and cars only made her feel more displaced. Marcus sat back down on the couch and waved the large Japanese man away. He bowed and left the room graciously to parts unknown.

"Ellen," Marcus said and paused. He stared down at the white tile. "Sweetheart. Angel. Love of my life."

He waited for a response, but Ellen didn't give him one. He rubbed his face with both hands and then kept speaking.

"You ever hear of the phenomenon called belief perseverance?" he asked while staring at the floor.

"Of course," she said, wiping the moisture from her face. "It's the documented psychological truth that people will continue to believe whatever they choose to, even in the face of irrefutable evidence of the contrary. So what? You're saying I'll never believe you?"

"On the contrary, my love. I'm hoping you will.

See, I'm praying that if you believe me, then you can convince the rest of America to believe me."

"Why the fuck do you keep calling me all these terms of endearment, you asshole? What the fuck is wrong with you?" Ellen belted out.

At that, Marcus walked over to Ellen and collapsed in front of her. He looked her directly in the eyes and gently took hold of her neck. "Eight years," Marcus said. "I spent eight years in prison because I loved you. You realize, Ellen Parker, you're the only girl I've ever loved to this day."

As he spoke, Ellen tried to retreat from his stare. As she wove and darted her eyes, Marcus always made sure to match her movements exactly. He never lost sight of the gorgeous, green eyes he fell in love with over a decade ago.

"You're the reason I exist, Ellen. There's no one to blame but yourself. But I still love you. I don't think I have any choice in the matter, really.

"But still, hell hath no fury like a teenager scorned," Marcus finished.

"Huh?" Ellen asked, confused.

"I've told you everything. Revealed to you the world. Broke down secret walls and even lightly hinted on how I hate what I do. But I'm gonna continue to do it. Why? Because this is now our bet. Prove to me to that people will believe what is right, not what is just in their heads. Prove me wrong, Ellen Parker. For the love of fucking God, prove me wrong."

".....how?" she asked, barely a whisper.

"I'm going to keep doing what I do. I'll live here, in this very apartment, fuck, I'll even give you the address. Tell the world about me. I'll keep blowing things up in America every couple of months, just like always. And what I want you to do is to take the information I've given you and stop me. I want you, with all the right in the universe, to stop something that technically doesn't even exist. I want you to end this."

"I don't understand," Ellen croaked. "If you don't

believe in it anymore, why not stop it yourself."

"Because," Marcus said and looked away from her. "You wanted a monster. And you made a monster. Eight years in prison for a crime committed out of love will do strange things to a man's brain."

Before Marcus could turn his face away, Ellen saw a tear form in the corner of her ex-boyfriend's eye.

"Stop me," Marcus said as he looked out the glass windows. "I'm like a kid with a fun, new smart phone. Hopelessly addicted. I've long lost the ability to stop myself. I need you to help me."

Ellen, in a frenzy, picked up the file and all its pages and darted for the front door. As she opened it, she took a quick glance back at the man who she once loved. She watched as he collapsed into a horrible pile of flesh and bone at the foot of a perfectly white ottoman. Holding the file with her left hand, she blew him a tender kiss with her right hand. She then paused to look at him one last time.

After Ellen slammed the door behind her, she never again saw Marcus Thomas face to face. He wrote her on several occasions, but she never replied. She was always too embarrassed.

This is because Ellen Parker-Johnson went on to be one of the highest-selling, non-fiction authors in America. She used every fact that Marcus gave her and even found some more of her own. Ellen was translated into thirteen languages throughout the world and her speaking events went from private auditoriums to stadiums.

But, forty years later, Buddhist terrorism was still the highest crime in the United States. In her lifetime, nothing had changed. She hadn't accomplished a thing. She lost their bet. Marcus couldn't be stopped.

One day, Ellen received a message that Marcus died; peacefully in his sleep from a stroke. She went upstairs to her study where she kept all her old books and notes. Opening the closet, she pulled a very old and worn chemistry book from off the shelf. She began flipping through the pages when she found an old photograph of two teenagers in love. Ellen smiled and thought of better days.

"You always were smarter than me, you asshole," she said through choked tears.

"Grandma, why are you crying?" a little girl of only ten years asked from the doorway behind Ellen.

"Oh, it's nothing, dear," she said as she wiped the tears from her eyes. Ellen put the photograph back into the textbook and the textbook back onto the shelf. "What is it, angel?"

"I just wanted to show you the new phone that dad got me. You know you can put it up to your forehead and it'll update your thoughts online without even typing? Come on! I wanna show you!" The little girl turned and ran toward the living room.

"Just had to rub it in, didn't you, you little shit?" Ellen asked as she looked up to the ceiling. "Maybe I'll figure out how to beat you in the next life, hm?" Ellen made her way out of the study, turning the light off as she closed the door.

Her last book was a quirky memoir she finished only a few months before she died. The book was dedicated to a man only known by the world as her high school ex-boyfriend.

It was called "I Never Much Cared for Cell Phones."

As Marcus opened to the dedication page, he smiled. "I knew you still loved me," he said aloud. He turned to the first page. "But I can't believe you still trusted everything the media told you, you dummy."

Marcus made himself comfortable on his white, leather couch and read the whole memoir in one sitting. When he finished it, he threw it into his fireplace. "That's for you, love." He watched the pages burn till there was nothing left but ash.

A SINGLE SENTENCE:

THE THREE WEDDINGS OF GALILEE

> *"And like Solomon and David, Jesus took upon himself several wives.*
> *For he was first wed to Joanna, then Susanna, and lastly to Magdalene*
> *When questioned by his followers in Judea, he spoke the words of Deuteronomy:*
> *A man may love many women, he said,*
> *So long as he does not love one more than another."*
> -The New Testament, Book of Luke, 95AD

I.

Genevieve Harrison quietly sits cross-legged in the studio green room. Smoothing her long, blue skirt, she looks at the television in front of her and watches as Jack McLaron yells into a video camera. His words are mostly unintelligible and overly abrasive. Even with his grey hair combed to one side and his clean, grey suit, he gives Genevieve the impression of being a local hero that somehow rose to national fame almost purely by accident. Using only her index finger to wave her blonde bangs away from her eyes, she briefly wonders why on earth she agreed to such an interview in the first place. As she continues to ponder this notion, her train of thought is suddenly broken when the door to the room swings open. A young man pokes his head through the gap and begins to speak.

"Seven minutes till you're on, Mrs. Harrison," he says. Genevieve takes a deep breath and stands up. She straightens out her jacket and walks confidently in the direction of her summoner.

"Let's get this over with," she whispers under her breath.

Genevieve follows the young man, an intern she presumes, onto the edge of the studio floor. She watches as Jack McLaron finishes his rant and tells the studio audience of the short, commercial break they'll be taking before resuming the show. In an act of obvious predetermined drama, he takes the pencil that he has been holding throughout his narration and throws it at the camera just before it cuts away.

I really do loathe this man, she thinks to herself.

Before she even realizes it, Jack McLaron is once again filming and he is calling her to join him on set. The audience stands up and claps, a response she knows has been pre-arranged, as she smiles and waves her way onto the brightly lit scene. Jack McLaron stands up and invites her to sit next to him - just on the other side of his desk - as though he actually desires such a thing. The two quickly seat and the audience regains its composure. The few people in the crowd who are actually aware of Genevieve Harrison's existence scoot just an inch forward on their hard, plastic chairs as they anticipate the interview.

"Well, Genevieve, thank you for joining us tonight," Jack begins to say.

"It's a pleasure, Jack," she says. They both know she's lying through her teeth. She puts her hands on his desk and is glad that there is a barrier, albeit slim, between herself and her host.

"Look, Genny, I'm not gonna beat around the bush," Jack begins to say. "You don't mind if I call you Genny, do you?" he finishes.

"No, of course not," Genevieve replies, even though she it's a nickname she's hated since childhood. Her fake smile continues to shine on her already wounded face.

"Good, so, Genny, I assume you've watched the show, right? I mean, I wanna cut right to the chase. This, uh, this husband of yours. Michael, I believe his name is?"

"Yes, yes, that's him," Genevieve says while nodding her head.

"Yes, so how does Mike feel about you wanting to take on a second husband?"

"Well, Michael supports me one hundred percent. We're of the same mind when it comes to women's rights. He doesn't see any reason why women shouldn't have the same rights as men when it comes to multiple spouses…"

"Wait, wait, let me ask you something. Do you even understand the dynamics of the American household?"

"Yes, yes I…" but Genevieve is cut off before she can finish.

"No, I don't think you do. You see, a man traditionally takes three wives not merely because it was deemed appropriate in the Bible, but because this way he can ensure the succession of the family's life and work with a proper heir. I mean, your average woman births what? Two or three kids? That's some rotten odds when you, as a mature adult, need to decide who's going to provide for everyone once you're gone. And that's why some men take nine wives; and I applaud them for it. They not only stick to that sacred number of three, but they get the satisfaction of knowing they'll get dozens of chances of having the perfect child to carry the family on. How can you – one woman married to multiple men – even remotely hope to carry out that mission? Are these men out of their minds?"

Genevieve moves her body forward and begins to open her mouth, but the crowd silences her when they stand and applaud. She wishes she could do more, but all she does is laugh nervously and subconsciously allow the capillaries in her face to fill with blood.

"Jack, if I may," she begins as the crowd quiets and sits back down.

"Of course," he says and gestures for her to continue.

"We don't believe in this archaic system that you've just described. Especially since it is a religious construct that has slowly weaved its way into our secular society. Even though eighty percent of the nation considers itself Christian, we both know only about half those people regularly attend church. Most people aren't even aware of where this societal structure even came from.

"But, anyway, Michael and I think that a personal legacy is all that's important; not what children you leave behind to inherit it. History has proven itself several times over that this fact remains true."

"Oh, God, you're not gonna start on this Charlemagne crap now, are you?" Jack asks with disgust.

"Why wouldn't I? He's a perfect example of a great king who had many wives and through his horrible choice, ended what could have been a great and long-lasting empire before it even got off the ground! How can you ignore it?"

"Because it's all hearsay and irrelevant. Especially when we know for a fact that the Roosevelt's gave us four great Presidents and three outstanding senators. How do you compete with that?"

As the crowd once again erupts into applause, Genevieve feels that pleading her case has now long passed the point of pointless. She simply disagrees with a slight movement of her head and debates which issue she wishes to press onto the unwilling commentator.

"What about the fact that nowhere in the Bible does Jesus actually discuss this family system you seem so dead-set on protecting?" Genevieve jabs back.

"I don't believe I follow you." Jack McLaron leans back and looks at her skeptically.

"There's no indication anywhere that Jesus married because he wanted to have some superior heir; it's clear that he took three wives because he loved three women. And, if that's the case then, honestly, why can't a woman love three men and want to take those men as husbands for herself? Why should she always be the one with a wife-in-law? If we were given the right to vote fifty years ago, I think it's time that the men understand that we are truly equals and therefore are capable of loving three men just as they are capable of loving three women."

In the audience, six women clap loudly and proudly. Two of them cry out in support. Genevieve turns to the crowd and laughs nervously. With the bright lights in her face, she can't see more than two feet in the direction of the shadowed crowd. She only nods in their direction as a gift of thanks.

"Mrs. Harrison," Jack begins and leans toward her, over his desk. "If God had wanted you to have three husbands, he would've given you three wombs."

"Mr. McLaron," Genevieve says as she leans in close to her opponent. "If God had wanted you to have three wives, he would've given you three penises." She smiles at him in a look of defiance; her left eyebrow cocked up high on her forehead. Several members of the audience chuckle.

At a loss for words, Mr. Jack McLaron merely smiles back at her.

II.

A large, stout, balding man named Thackeray Morstead walks into the front door of his apartment and shouts out "I'm home!" His already loosened tie is now being undone completely by his left hand as he walks through the foyer and into the family room.

"Hi, dear," Donna, his second wife, says as she approaches him from the far hallway. Two knitting needles adorn her auburn hair; gorgeous locks which spend most of their time pulled back into a ponytail so as not to bother her while she sews. Happy to see her husband home from his long day of work, she smiles and kisses him tenderly.

As they separate, he looks over to the couch and sees one of his daughters, Emma, seated comfortably and watching the television. Briefly, he glances at the glowing screen to see if he approves of the content. A fairly attractive woman in a rather professional-looking navy blue skirt-suit sits on the left-hand side of the screen. On the right, at the far side of a small desk, sits a well known political pundit of increasing age and of which Thackeray has never been a big fan. The woman he does not recognize.

"Emma, sweetie, turn that garbage off. Why on earth would a girl of your tender age even bother with that nonsense?" he asks.

"But dad!" she says in protest and turns around. "Genevieve Harrison is on and my teacher, Miss Shore, is always talking about her. She sounds really cool. And I'm thirteen and am old enough to watch whatever I want!"

Just then, Thackeray's wife Michelle walks in from the kitchen. She wears an apron on top of her simple, white dress. Her hands are damp — a sign that they've just been washed — though a few spots of white flour still decorate her strong arms. "Hi honey, how was work?" She stands a few inches away from him and only connects her lips to his cheek so as not to soil his clothes.

"Oh, just fine, I suppose. Same as always," he says and smiles. Emma turns around and goes back to watching TV, hoping she hasn't missed anything important. "And you, Shell?"

"Just more of the same for me, too. Of course, I did find out at the store today that the price of flour went up another twenty-five cents per pound."

"Again?" he asks, agitated. "That's the second time this year." Michelle only raises her arms and looks to the side. Her actions suggest the phrase 'but what can you do?' Thackeray sighs.

It's then that four boys and two girls come running down the hallway. "Dad!" they all scream in unison. Michelle and Donna each take a step back as the children of various ages crowd around their father. A large, group hug is formed as he kisses each one of their foreheads. Special attention goes to a boy of eleven years; Thackeray winks at his son, Roland, and ruffles his unkempt mop of dirty blonde hair. The older son of twelve notes this behavior in jealous silence.

Slowly stepping out into the living room is Thackeray's third and youngest wife, Cassandra. Crossing her arms, she smiles at the scene and leans against the wall. Still with his children around him, Thackeray looks over at the young woman and smiles. She closes her eyes and kisses the air in his direction. As she opens her eyelids, Thackeray is briefly lost in the hypnotizing power of her bright blue eyes. Cassandra blushes and turns to the side. Aware of her husband's seemingly single-minded behavior, Donna loudly clears her throat. Thackeray shakes his head as if coming out of a trance.

"So, right, um, what's for dinner tonight?" he asks Michelle.

"Lasagna, garlic bread, and green beans," she tells him. Six of Thackeray's children are excited by this announcement. Emma, still seated on the couch, remains unaware of the menu.

"Okay, so has everyone finished their homework?" he asks the offspring before him. Even though all of them nod their heads in agreement, a few of them are hesitant.

"Rachel," Thackeray tells his middle daughter. "Don't make me check over your homework." She rolls her eyes at the comment and turns around to make her way back into the bedroom she shares with her two sisters.

"Cassandra, do you mind helping me with something in my room before dinner?" Thackeray asks his wife.

"Of course not," she replies. "Don't be long." With that, she turns and walks delicately back down the apartment hallway. Her thick, black hair waves at him enticingly as it brushes against her slim back. The curved tips of her locks intermingle with the fabric belt around her hips. For a brief moment, Thackeray's heart rate noticeably increases. He draws in a breath.

Later that night, long after they've all finished dinner and Thackeray's seven children are all in bed and asleep, his first wife, Michelle, exits her husband's personal bathroom. Now clean of all kitchen-related smears and blemishes, she wears only a light pink, cotton night gown; Donna had made it by hand for one of Michelle's birthdays a few years back.

Michelle approaches the far side of the queen-sized bed. She moves the covers aside and slips herself between the soft sheets. Thackeray is already present and is comfortably reading the latest issue of Time magazine by the light of his desk lamp. Michelle sits upright and leans against the headboard. Her eyes are occupied by a long, dark hair that curls slightly at one end. It rests neatly atop Thackeray's beige quilted blanket. Gazing at the strand, her fingers attack each other's cuticles in nervous, fidgeting motions. Thackeray doesn't seem to notice. Finally, Michelle takes a deep and weighted breath before sliding down into her husband's bed.

As she moves deeper into the cool bedding, Michelle rolls over and puts her hand on her husband's leg. Slowly and delicately, she begins to run her fingertips back and forth along his thigh. She nudges her face lightly against his arm and closes her eyes. Thackeray merely continues to read his article on the ongoing threat of European socialism. His only acknowledgement to his wife's actions is a slight raise in the left corner of his mouth. Some might call it an arrogant smirk.

"Not tonight, honey," he says without looking at her. "Long day at the office. Maybe next time, hm?" He leans over and kisses her forehead. Without waiting for her acquiescence, Thackeray returns to his literature. Michelle's eyes snap open and she takes a deep breath before pulling away from her husband of fifteen years.

"Thackeray?" she asks him. She remains completely horizontal.

"Yes, dear?" he replies.

"Can we talk for a moment?" A barely noticeable amount of slightly salty liquid begins to fill up her eyes.

"About anything you like." He casually continues to read.

"Why is it okay for a man to have three wives?" she asks.

"Excuse me?" Thackeray finally looks in his wife's direction, but continues to hold the magazine in his hand.

Michelle stoically repeats herself. "Why is it okay for a man to have three wives?"

"Well, why not?" he replies. "That's a silly question. When has it ever *not* been okay for a man to have three wives? Why not ask me why....bricks are red?"

"It's not the same and you know it," she says and props herself up a bit.

"Then I have to say that I don't know what you mean," Thackeray says and finally puts down his magazine onto his lap. He sinks down slightly to be at a better eye-level with his wife before continuing. "Every man has three wives. Everyone at the office does. All your girlfriends have two other wives-in-law to their one husband. Why is it okay? I suppose because that's just the way things are? Or cause we don't live in India? Is that the answer you were looking for?"

Michelle swallows and chooses her words carefully before speaking.

"Even though everyone seems to forget this detail, the stipulation that men can have many wives is that he loves each one equally."

"Well, of course. I mean, that goes without sayi…"

"Equally," Michelle interrupts her husband with conviction.

"I know, Shell. Equally." Thackeray's voice takes on a hint of timidity in fear of where his wife is directing the conversation.

Still looking her husband in the eyes, she bluntly tells him, "We haven't made love in nearly a year."

"That's ridiculous," he says, pulling his head back for emphasis. "I mean, it was just the other week when…" and he trails off in his recollection.

"The other week, right? When Sophia had her dance recital? You mean in October? You do realize this is July, don't you?" Michelle sits up a bit as her husband's responses agitate her more and more.

"I…I didn't even realize. Um…" Thackeray staggers.

"In that time period, do you even have the vaguest clue how many times you and Cassie have jumped in bed together? And in the middle of the day when you're children are still awake, no less?"

"Michelle, angel," he looks up at her and into her watery, brown eyes. "That doesn't mean I love you any less. I just love you…differently."

"Differently?!" Michelle now sits up completely. "Differently?! You're supposed to love us the same! Shit, I knew you'd say something stupid like that. Lord, you're incredible." She uses her shoulder to wipe a tear away from her eye.

"Something like what? I…"

"Just shut up," she tells him. Thackeray quickly silences himself. "I've thought about this for a while now. I wanted to at least talk with you first to see if you'd defend yourself or apologize. Ha, apologize. What was I thinking? That'd be the first time you'd ever apologized for something in your life."

"React what way? What have you been thinking about?" Thackery shrinks back under the covers. He's never seen his wife in such a fervor. "Where is all this coming from?"

"Open your eyes, Thackery. It's coming from everywhere. Genevieve Harrison is right. Women are treated like a lesser species. Of course, you probably haven't even bothered to take the time to look into what a woman has to say," she says with contempt.

"Michelle, what exactly are you trying to say?"

She looks down at him and scowls. "Thackeray, I want a divorce."

"What?" he says in disbelief. "That's ridiculous. Look, honey, I'm sure we can work this out. People only get divorced in severe circumstances. We can…"

"Not anymore. This is a new world, Thackeray Delano Morstead. One you'll have to learn to get used to. I'm leaving you." She takes a deep breath and lets it out in nervous stutters. "And I'm taking our three children with me."

"But you can't!" Thackeray suddenly becomes panic stricken and sits up. "There's no way you'll be allowed to do that!"

"I can and I will," she returns calmly. "I've been looking into this for the past couple of months. In between preparing your meals, of course. Don't worry, soon you can expect me to be out of your life forever." Michelle looks Thackeray in the eyes. "And Roland, too."

Thackeray sinks down into his bed. He's sure his heart will stop beating at any moment.

III.

"Whiskey and soda," Jerry Thomas says to the bartender. In a few quick motions of the hand, a drink is made and given to Jerry. A monetary exchange takes place between the two individuals. Jerry leaves a tip on the bar before walking away and sliding into the banquette of a small table near the bar's back corner. As he takes a sip, he glances up at one of the bar's several television sets. A baseball game is shown, but being neither interested in the teams that are playing nor in the score, he turns his eyes elsewhere and his thoughts as well.

Eventually, a girl with short blonde hair and a few lines of stress around her eyes enters the lounge and looks around. Since it is only 4pm and the establishment is mostly unpopulated, she easily catches sight of Jerry when he holds up his right hand and waves slightly in her direction. She casually walks over to the table while removing her long overcoat. Tossing the coat over a chair, she drops her purse down onto the small table and begins to rummage around through it.

"Sorry, I'm late," Alison says as she finds her elusive wallet. "How long you been here?"

"Oh, not too long, Miss Shore. This is still my first one," Jerry says, acknowledging his empty drink.

Alison grimaces and makes a sound of disgust. "Geez, you know I hate it when you call me that. What are you drinking?" she asks her friend.

"Whiskey and soda," Jerry replies while shrugging. "Same as always."

"K, be right back," she says and approaches the bar. She soon returns and sits down on the hard, wooden, bar chair with two cocktails in hands.

"So how've you been? How's school?" he asks the second question in a slightly mocking tone.

"Oh, it's okay," she says in an exhalation of breath. "These kids' minds are just so messed up though. Even in middle school, I sometimes feel like I'm teaching kindergarten."

"Ah, still fighting the good fight, I see," Jerry says and chuckles. He follows the comment with a sip of his drink.

"Always," Alison says slyly.

"Ah, ever my little crusader." Jerry raises his glass to Alison. "And how do all these parents feel about you filling their children's minds with your left-wing, liberal, feminist manifesto?"

"Well, I haven't heard much from the parents themselves, so far. I mostly just get one or two kids saying 'But Miss Shore, my dad says what you told us last week was a bunch of hippy garbage.' Though that's to be expected, I suppose."

"I suppose," Jerry echoes. He rolls his eyes and looks off to the side.

"What?" Alison cries out defensively.

"Hey, I didn't say anything!"

"No, but I've known you for well over a decade, Jerry Thomas. That look and that tone of voice mean that something else is going on in that big, mysterious brain of yours. You can't make a living doing what you do without bringing home a little of the crazy. Or do suddenly all those offbeat and, somehow successful, comic books publish themselves? C'mon. Out with it."

Jerry sighs and, using his straw, plays with the ice in his drink. He doesn't look up at Alison. "You sure you really wanna hear what I have to say?"

"Of course I do." She looks at him questioningly. "Well, you're not against me, are you?"

"Not exactly," he says, still stirring his drink.

"You're against me? You think that men should have all the power…"

"Hey!" Jerry yells out but then quickly quiets back down. "Calm down will you? I don't think that and you know it." He sits up and hunches over the table in order to be within closer speaking range of his friend.

"Then what?"

"Did you watch McLaron the other night? When Genevieve Harrison was on?"

"Of course I did."

"Was there any part of the interview that struck you as," he pauses for a brief moment. "As particularly interesting?"

"I can think of several parts, personally."

"What about the part when they discuss the quantities of male and female genitalia on any given individual?"

"That was by far the funniest part, yes," Alison says and laughs, remembering the banter. "But interesting? Not really."

"You didn't notice how they were both right?"

"What! How do you figure? Harrison totally put him in his place," she says, defending her idol.

"Not saying she didn't. But in a sense, so did he. He was just as right as she was. It was only cause she got the last word that she seemed on top. If that transaction happened in the opposite way, with her going first, he would have equally been right and the audience would have gone ballistic."

"Are you saying that men and women have equal rights? Cause if so, then I don't know why we're having this conversation."

"For the love of…" Jerry trails off and readjusts his posture. Taking a sip from his drink, he finally continues. "Alison, do you have three wombs?"

"I don't see what that has…"

"Just answer the question," he interrupts passively.

"No. No, I do not." She rolls her eyes as she answer..

"Okay. And do I have three penises? Or, better question, does any man have three penises?"

"Not to my knowledge."

"So then both parties are wrong. What I got from the interview is something that no one else seemed to get. That no one should have three husbands and no one should have three wives. Or any multiple spouses, for that matter. The whole system is actually ridiculous. We were each meant to have one spouse and that's it."

"Oh, Jerry, now you're just being absurd."

"Says the girl who's a strong proponent of changing the face of the entire family unit as we know it."

"Well, yeah," Alison begins. "But I just want to

level the playing field. What you're talking about is gutting the entire economic and social structure of our society and starting from scratch."

"Just because something is fundamentally broken doesn't mean we shouldn't bother fixing it."

"But what you want is a fantasy, Jerry."

"Oh, so, what? Small revolutions in the name of women are acceptable? But large revolutions that help *both* sexes are fantasy?"

"Okay, I think this is getting a bit more intense than either of us realize. Let's…"

Just then, the volume on the television is turned up to an exceedingly loud level. Jerry and Alison both look up from each other to the vibrantly tuned vacuum tubes attached to the bar walls. They quickly notice how the programming has switched from that of baseball to that of news. An elegantly dressed gentleman graces the screen and orally dictates the text he is being shown for his viewing audience.

"…still unsure as to what exactly happened. All we know is that Genevieve Harrison, one of the primary leaders of the growing Marriage Equality for Women movement, has been shot in an attempted assassination by a currently unknown gunman. Our reports tell us that she was leaving a restaurant in Boston when suddenly a shot was heard from across the street and that is when Genevieve collapsed onto the sidewalk. We don't have much else right…I'm sorry, just one second…I'm…I'm being told we have a pedestrian video of the shooting…But, viewers please be warned…I'm being told it's very graphic and you may want to turn away from your TV set."

The shot cuts abruptly from that of the stately organized newsroom to that of a shaky street filmed with extremely poor film quality. At first, the image is of three boys of slightly varying single-digit ages running around in broad daylight. As they play on the sidewalk, a female voice from off camera abruptly asks, "Hey, is that Genevieve

Harrison?" The camera suddenly shifts focus from that of the children to that of three individuals exiting a restaurant across the street. "Hey, yeah it is," the male camera operator says. In the center is Genevieve Harrison. Both her sides are flanked by well-dressed men.

Suddenly, a loud gunshot is heard and the left-side of Genevieve's neck simply explodes in a firework display of blood. The red liquid covers the face of the man to her left as she falls backward onto the ground. The camera shakes during the whole ordeal but amazingly never loses focus. "Oh my God, Oh my God, Oh my God," is all the male camera operator says. The same female voice from off camera shrieks and in a quick blur of movement, we see the camera spin back to the three children as their mother runs to hold them in her arms. Just as fast it turned away, the camera returns to the focus of the restaurant and the scene bounces up and down as the spectator runs over to get a closer look. As a perfect shot of Genevieve Harrison lying on the cement with a massive pool of blood pouring from her neck comes into view, the other of Genevieve's men looks up at the camera. "What the fuck are you doing?" he asks. Before a response can be given, the man stands up and says, "Turn that damn thing off!" One of his hands makes a long, sweeping motion at the camera and the picture quickly blacks out.

For five-point-three seconds, the channel remains blank as the studio editors try to decide on how to proceed. For Alison, Jerry and twenty million other Americans, each second ticks by like an epoch.

"Ladies and gentlemen," the news announcer says when he finally returns. His face is white and his normally calm demeanor is shaken. "I don't mean to make guesses, but it appears Genevieve Harrison – prominent political figure in the Marriage Equality movement – has been mortally wounded. I...I think it is safe to say that she has been assassinated. I..." he pauses, unsure of what to say next. Stunned, nervous and well-versed in what happens when political revolutionaries are assassinated, he

accidentally lets slips out the only words on his mind.
"May God help us all."

IV.

James Earl Maddox sits and stares contemplatively at the chess pieces in front of him. After a time, he picks up the black rook and moves it three spaces to the right. He places it down on the board and then quietly stares again as he goes over all the possible outcomes of the game in his head. In thought, he scratches his graying temple. He does his best to ignore his other companions in the game room; all of which share his same attire of a clean, white jumpsuit.

Across the rec room, a heavily-barred door opens. Through it steps a young man wearing semi-formal attire and with a notebook and pen. He shakes the hand of the orderly who closes the door quickly. James looks up at the man briefly, but then refocuses his attention on the one-man chess game before him. Through the top of his eyes, James sees the outsider adjust his clothes before slowly making his way over to his table.

"James Earl Maddox?" the young man says as he approaches.

"That's me," James says with a heavy Southern drawl as he adjusts his black, plastic glasses. He maintains his focus on the chess board before him. "Course no one ever called me by my full name till…Well, you know. I assume you're from that newspaper, correct?"

"The New Spectator, yes. I'm glad you allowed me this interview, Mr. Maddox. My name is Christopher Scott."

"Nice to meet you, Mr. Scott," James says casually as he looks up from his chess game and holds out his right hand. The two shake and James can feel the rigid tension in Christopher's body when their hands meet.

"So, Mr. Scott, if I'm not mistaken, your newspaper only has a circulation of about twenty thousand people, is that not correct?" James asks.

"Twenty thousand and growing, Mr. Maddox. Why do you ask?" Christopher replies.

"Oh, no reason. You mind if I continue to play during the interview?" the elderly man asks as he finally looks up at his companion and smiles. "I do love a good game of chess."

"Of course, please," the reporter says and gestures to the plastic game pieces. James places his elbow on the table and returns his attention to the gameboard. "May I begin?"

"Whenever you like," James says without looking up. From his messenger bag, Christopher pulls out a pad and pen

"Before I start, I just want to go over a few basic facts. Just to get the details from the horse's mouth, so to speak." Christopher laughs nervously but James doesn't seem to notice.

"Right, so, you're from West Virginia, is that correct?"

"Born and raised," replies James. He picks up and moves a pawn on the chess board.

"I also have that you never married nor had any children. You lived a mostly solitary life before your arrest, no?"

"All true, so far as I'm aware."

"And instead of attending college, you went to work on your uncle's corn farm after high school, no? Worked there until your arrest?"

"Sure do have your facts straight," James says nonchalantly.

"Now, you may not have ever attended college, but I did find a particularly interesting paper you wrote in high school," Christopher says. "About Marxist theory and its application to the capitol economy of Asia. I found it in an old box of files your sister let me look through. Despite what the other reports had said about her, I found her to be quite accommodating."

James looks up at the reporter through the top of his glasses and sheds a slight smile. "Well, I gave her a call and let her know you'd be coming. Asked her to be a little more helpful, on my behalf. And I was hoping you'd find some of that old nonsense. Good work."

Christopher smiles. "Thank you, Mr. Maddox."

"So, you actually read the thing?"

"Of course! I found it quite interesting and indicative of your…"

"Oh, don't give me any of that garbage. You and I both know it was a load of pig shit. But imagine you didn't know me or nothing about me. What kind of person would you have made me out to be, just by reading that paper? You figure me out yet?"

"Well," Christopher begins and blushes. "I don't know if I figured you out. But, honestly, Mr. Maddox, the paper seemed to come from a social revolutionary. You, yourself, seemed to be quite the ideal extremist in your younger days."

"I suppose you could say that," James says and smiles.

"So what happened?" Christopher asks abruptly.

"What happened?" James asks and looks up at his interviewer, confused. His eyebrows cross reflexively.

"Yes, you seemed to go from idealistic radical in your younger years to stout conservative in your elder years; to the point of committing assassination of a revolutionary figure, no less. You seemed to turn to the opposite side of the coin, no? I'm just curious to know what happened to change your heart."

James Earl Maddox takes a deep breath and grunts. He turns back toward his chess game and seems suddenly aggravated with his interviewer. "Yeah. Suppose I did."

"You seem upset by my supposition." Christopher pauses and thinks. "Are you saying you're *not* conservative? Do you see yourself as a revolutionary for being an assassin?"

"Lord, you're a fool," James says. He closes his eyes and shakes his head. "But no, I don't suppose I consider myself a conservative."

"Then why murder Genevieve Harrison? Why assassinate the star of the liberal movement?"

"For reasons you clearly aren't capable of understanding," James says and once again goes back to his chess game. "If you were at all, you'd be asking me slightly more directed questions. Guess I was just wrong this time. Can't be right all the time, I suppose."

"More directed? How do you mean?" Christopher asks.

"Oh, so you want me to tell you how to interview me now?"

"Please, sir, Mr. Maddox. Just give me something – anything – to help me understand why you would murder someone if you weren't against them?"

James takes his glasses off and drops them hard onto the table. Christopher flinches noticeably.

"Fine, but this is all you get. Then, this little piss poor excuse of an interview is over. You're lucky I liked the article you wrote about why a Buddhist would make the best U.S. president or you wouldn't even get this much." James clears his throat and scratches his temple again. "So, how many people believed in Genevieve Harrison's cause before I did what I did?" James asks.

"Roughly fifteen percent of the nation, give or take," Christopher responds quickly having prepared extensively for this interview.

"And how many afterwards? How many now?"

"I guess it's about half now. The legislation they're trying to pass in Congress has a pretty even army on both sides. Not to mention the people in other countries, too, where she's become a symbol for worldwide change. That's why I couldn't believe you'd grant me this…Wait…Are you saying you killed her because you knew it would increase her popularity?"

James Earl Maddox shrugs his shoulders. He moves the white bishop diagonally four spaces to the left.

"You can't be serious, though. There's no way you could have foreseen the country's reaction and the repercussions that followed."

James shrugs his shoulders again and remains focused on the game.

"And even if you somehow could, you would have fought to clear your name. In fact, your plea of insanity rather lends itself to the notion that everything you've told me is some elaborately concocted story. I think you're really in here because this is exactly where you belong," Christopher says being half-honest and half-rash hoping to illicit a reaction from his interviewee.

James shrugs his shoulders for a third time. "Yup, that's right," he begins. "Just some stupid redneck who hates change."

It's then that the proper neuron in Christopher Scott's brain fires and causes him to realize that James Earl Maddox's story is entirely too true. The understanding is accompanied by the revelation that James would have to play the part of a bigot - for life - else people would know that the assassination was a tactical ploy which would completely neutralize its effects.

For a time, Christopher sits in silence and stares blankly at the list of questions on his notebook, all of which now seem irrelevant. James Earl Maddox continues to play chess as though unaffected by the current situation. He does, however, wave one of his arms effectively summoning one of the hospital orderlies. The orderly approaches, places a hand on Christopher's shoulder, and tells him it's time to go.

Walking away, Christopher's thoughts are in flux. Dozens of questions and comments flip through his mind as he walks away from the most important figure he's ever had the honor of interviewing. Impulsively, he turns around and blurts out one last comment.

"You know, Jack McLaron is one of your biggest

supporters. He says that you're a reminder that people always get what's coming to them."

James Earl Maddox looks up and smiles. "If you ever meet him, tell him that's exactly what I'm hoping for."

A SINGLE SENTENCE

THE TENTH CRUSADE

> *"Therefore, your Worship should know that it has pleased us to heavily increase all punishments concerning the Christians and now any one of these who wishes to observe Christian religion may do so only upon pain of death on that person and their families."*
> -The Edict of Milan, Constantine the Great, 313AD

I.

Malcolm stood outside the cavern of the Oracle and trembled. Even though it was only mid-September, there was a cruel wind ripping its way off the Atlantic Ocean and straight through Malcolm's body. He felt a shiver run up his spine as he flipped the black hood of his sweater up, over his head. Then he took a slow, icy breath and stepped into the dark, forbidding cave of the Oracle of Babylon.

Casually, Malcolm walked through the cave and mostly ignored the various murals and runes on the rock walls. He kept his head down as he passed hundreds, if not thousands, of black wax candles situated within the walls and on the floor of the granite cavern. The dark wax ran down the rock walls and formed Styxian rivers in the slowly building heat of the Oracle's cave. These thick rivers mixed with white chalk; with smeared goat's blood; with gold flakes and old incense; with sea salt and ions to create the strangest and most unique scenery one could imagine.

Even on their death bed, people were still able to intimately describe even the most impeccable details of the Oracle's cave.

Though none of this really fazed Malcolm. He simply continued to stroll down the path of rock and sand, deeper into the dark cave. He kept his head down and concentrated hard on the question he'd been wanting to ask the Oracle for days now. For weeks. Maybe even months.

It was all he had thought about. It was almost an obsession.

Eventually, Malcolm came to the Gateway. He wrapped his arms around his body and looked up at the centuries old doorway that separated the Mundane world from that of the Arcane. It was a centuries-old slab of wood, black as pitch and half-petrified. A bizarre, indecipherable language was carved into every inch of the Gateway that glowed an unearthly pale blue by means of a luminescent oil. Past the strange, ancient Gateway, Malcolm was no longer in the world of mortals. Once he crossed this threshold, he was in the presence of the Oracle.

An agent of the immortals. The voice of the Goddess Athena.

Malcolm took a deep breath and stepped through the Gateway. He was immediately greeted by a blast of warm, white, humid air. The Oracle's Vapor was a naturally occurring "steam" that arose from a crack in the earth. It was this vapor that not only allowed the Oracle to predict the future, but also for the layperson to accept the cryptic prediction of the Oracle. It was distinctly similar to the Native American practice of sharing tobacco smoke in order to share one's thoughts and feelings.

Without the Vapor, there could be no psychic connection. Therefore, there could be no predictions. The Vapor was why this small spot of Earth held an Oracle to begin with. There were only six known vents of Vapor known to exist in the world and this small town in Long Island, New York was one of them. In their own ways, these naturally occurring zeniths were more important than the Oracles themselves.

Malcolm immediately felt himself get lightheaded from the Vapor. He expected it though. After all, this wasn't his first time visiting the Oracle of Babylon. Hell, it wasn't even his tenth. He was long used to the effects of the Oracle's Vapor; something that few people could say they had experienced even once. A visit to the Oracle, after all, was a visit with a very high price tag and only a select few could afford it.

After a few moments, Malcolm put his head back down and continued to walk. Soon, he found what he was looking for among the thick, white vapor and dark, rough stone. At the top of Malcolm's peripheral vision were the bottom rungs of a simple wooden stool. Resting on the bottom rung were a naked pair of feet that were anything but simple. Legs followed those bare feet. Perfect, flawless legs the color of cream and winter. They were covered in a dress made of gossamer and spider silk. Looking closely at the fabric, one could see everything and nothing beneath the dress's thin, delicate layers.

Looking further up from the Oracle's legs was agony. Her feet were perfect enough. Her legs alone were immaculate expressions of torture. But once you got to her hips. To her waist. To her neck....

There were people who wrote whole books about the Oracle. They wrote whole series. They got one look at the Oracle of Babylon and were changed for life. Thirty years would go by and they couldn't look at people the same way ever again. Couldn't focus. Couldn't handle real life.

Her white filament dress barely covered her

unnaturally perfect body. Her blonde hair fell down in curls around her pouty lips and her icy blue eyes. There was no aspect of the Oracle that didn't reek of godly perfection. It was virtually – painfully – impossible not to gaze upon her and think that somehow, somewhere above you there were Gods. Dozens of Gods. Hundreds of them. Looking down upon humanity and plotting and thinking and conniving and wondering how they could help us and wondering how they could hurt us.

But the Oracle of Babylon sat in her cavern upon her tripod, inhaling the Vapor of the earth, and few could look upon her and not say a prayer. Behind her stood six Acolytes all dressed in red robes, ready to carry out the Oracle's every order. They were young girls who all hoped that, one day, they would become the Oracle when the Fates called for such an event to occur.

Malcolm stood in the Oracle's presence and held out his open palms. His hood still over his head and his eyes still focused on the ground, he choked back a smile and began to ask his question.

"Oracle," he began, speaking gruffly. "May I have an audience?"

"You come with no gift?" the Oracle asked. "No token of your appreciation?"

"My gift will be understood once my question is asked," he said. The Oracle paused and considered this.

"Continue," she said, her voice a mixture of dandelions and butterfly wings. "What do you ask of the Gods?"

Malcolm coughed and regained his composure. "It's quite simple." He took a deep breath and then asked his great question.

"I'd really like to put my dick in your mouth tonight. Think that'll happen?"

The Oracle stood up in disbelief, her jaw nearly falling to the ground. The Oracle never stood up. Ever. To speak this way to Her wasn't even punishable by death, it was simply unheard of. There was no precedence for this.

She took a step forward as she began to organize her thoughts. Opening her mouth to speak, the Oracle was silenced by one of her Acolytes.

One of her Acolytes quickly became two. Then three. Then all six of them were laughing their asses off.

Stunned and speechless, the Oracle turned to face the young, hooded girls behind her. "What on earth is happening here?" she asked in a strong, Southern accent as she abandoned her vocal training.

That's when Malcolm threw his hood back and stood up straight. "Hey, sugar. How's the prophecy business going?"

The Oracle took one look at Malcolm and let a small scream of joy escape from her esophagus. "Oh my god!" she belted out. But then she thought for another second and turned around to look at her entourage. "Wait, you all knew about this?" she asked angrily yet playfully.

"Come on, Karly," one of the Acolytes said. "It's Malcolm. How could we not go along with it?"

For two or three seconds, the Oracle of Babylon was pissed. But then she acquiesced and turned back to Malcolm. She smiled. "How long have you been planning this?" she asked.

"I don't know. Girls, what's it been? Like three, maybe four hours?"

"What?" Karly asked as she walked up to him and punched him in the chest. "You're such an asshole."

"Oh, Gods knows that's the truth," he said as he put his hands on the Oracle's hips. "You miss me?"

"Eh," Karly said with a sly smile as she put her arms around Malcolm's neck. "Only a little. I mean, I've been single for what? Two days now?"

"A wonder you haven't killed yourself in that time without me." He smiled the dickish grin Karly had come to know and love.

Karly chuckled. "How are you so full of yourself?"

"Come on, how many guys on the planet can say they've brought the Oracle of Babylon to pure ecstasy?"

"Strong words, sailor," she said as she kissed Malcolm on the mouth. "Plus, you know that number is way higher than you pretend it is. Let's try not to forget that before I was worshipped while sitting on this old stool, I was worshipped while dancing on a pole. God, can you imagine what would happen if one of the dozens of guys that paid for my full service Champagne Room experience recognized me in here? Talk about awkward…"

"Hush, hush. Don't ruin the fantasy for me. And anyway, I'm still the best sex you've ever had. Or did you tell that to all the guys at the strip club, too?"

"Wouldn't you like to know," she said as she bit his ear. "Oh, and extremely high." That's when Karly jumped up and wrapped her legs around Malcolm's waist. "My room is over there," she said as she pointed to her left and nibbled on Malcolm's ear.

"I think you meant moderately high, dear. We both know this vapor is mostly just water with only the slightest amount of mind-altering chemicals."

"No, silly," the Oracle said, whispering in Malcolm's ear. "I was giving you the answer to your question."

A brief wave of confusion washed over Malcolm's face. Then he remembered what his question had been and he promptly perked up, both literally and figuratively. "Ahhhh, well then. Excuse me, ladies," Malcolm said to the Acolytes. "But I need to make this Oracle scream about the Gods." With that, he carried Karly into her personal bedchamber and closed the door.

The Acolytes soon dispersed. They all believed Malcolm. And none of them really wanted to stick around to hear the auditory proof.

II.

"Well, so I guess you've been sleeping with Karly again then, eh?" Rami asked.

"What makes you say that?" Malcolm replied, smirking.

"Several things really. First of all, you haven't complained once about how long it's been since you've gotten laid. Second, the last time I saw you a month ago, you told me Karly and her most recent boyfriend were on the rocks. And third of all, we're heading to a bar to meet a few of my friends and you haven't once asked me if there's any girls there that might be interested in you."

Malcolm burst out laughing. "I swear to the Gods, they've been teaching you some clever shit out there at Langley. Even though I still can't believe you sold out and took a government job. Vagina."

"Yeah," Rami said and smiled. "Can't win em all."

A strong wind suddenly ripped its way down 1st Avenue and Malcolm wrapped his coat around his body. Rami didn't seem much fazed by it. "Hell, what's with this 20-degree weather in early October?" Malcolm asked. "This fall has been bullshit."

"Ah, be a man and deal with it," Rami said and paused. "Hey, and speaking of being a man, doesn't Karly ever worry you?"

"Huh?" Malcolm asked. "How so? Cause she's an Oracle? I mean, yeah, that's weird and all. But I've known her for like ten years now. When we met each other, we were teenagers."

"No, not that stupid crap. Don't you worry she might actually fall for you one day?"

"Oh, Gods no. We've been on and off sex buddies since forever. Yeah, we dated for like six months when we first met, but that's old history. She's had something like a half-dozen boyfriends and I've had…well…maybe like two girlfriends since then. But that's cause I have serious emotional problems, as you're well aware. But we've never once considered that what we're doing together is more than just a really good time."

"You're absolutely sure of that?"

"Positive," Malcolm said. "And why are you so worried about Karly and I all of the sudden? You know exactly how drop dead gorgeous she is.

"Oh, no argument, son," Rami said. He chuckled as he reached for the door of the bar they were going into. "But the difference is that she's the fucking Oracle of Babylon. I'd probably try to marry the girl."

"So what?" Malcolm said as he entered the bar. "Every guy on the planet is."

"Except for you, Malcolm. And it really worries me what might happen if she ever realized that. What happens if she falls in love with you and you don't love her back? What happens if you scorn an Oracle? Shit, man. That scares the crap out of me."

"Fair enough," Malcolm said and slapped Rami on the back. "But you wanna hear a secret?"

"Uh, Gods do I ever."

"Okay, well, Karly isn't a Romanus anymore. She's converted."

Rami came to a dead stop in the bar's doorway and put a hand against Malcolm's chest, stopping him dead in his tracks. He looked him square in the eyes. "Are you sure?"

"Of course I'm…"

"No, Mal, I'm not fucking with you. Are you sure that the Oracle's converted? You're telling me right now, on pain of death, that she's a Christian?"

"Okay, well, that's an overly fucking serious way of putting it and I'm sure your blood-hatred of Christians might have something to do with that, but yeah. We've had more than one talk about it. She's a Christian. Half the prophecies she tells to people are actually just verses out of the Christian Bible, if you can believe it. So, no. I'm not worried what she might do to me. I'm far more worried what the Department of Foresight might do to her if they ever heard about what her true religion was. Even if the girl was in love with me, I'm pretty sure it's now in her code to forgive me and all that."

Rami took a deep breath. "Okay, man. I'm sorry. Don't worry about it."

"You sure? Cause your new job has me a little weirded out. And I'm not sure if you more or less threatening my life over Karly being a Christian is cause you've been sort of a racist bastard when it comes to Christians ever since the day I met you or cause of this scary ass new job of yours."

Rami sighed. "Look, this CIA gig definitely has me a bit spooked. Do I have a general dislike of the Christian mentality? Sure. I mean, that's probably why I got hired in the first place. All this Tenth Crusade nonsense going on is more intense than you know. I…We need to know who's Christian and who isn't. Let's not forget, we're at war, Mal. But hell, the Third Civil War is one of these new, modern wars where few people actually ever fight or get killed. Wars were easier to fight back then. When one team ran out of people, the war was over. Now? Now it's subversion, spies, government leverage, and media all being used as arsenal.

"Think about it," Rami continued. "What would happen if the government decided to go to Karly for help and backing. If she's really a Christian, that could go pretty fucking horribly. Not to mention the sort of damage she could do to our efforts to squash the demands of the Tenth Crusade. If she started to publicly rally for Christians, it'd be a shitstorm. We're not giving those Jesus-worshipping peace-freaks their own sovereign nation. Not now and not ever. This is the sort of shit the people I work for need to know about."

"Well, that escalated quickly," Malcolm said with wide, frightened eyes. "Are you sure you're even allowed to be talking like this with me? Am I gonna die in my sleep later for this whole conversation?"

Rami laughed. "Hey, you think any of that was a state secret? Come on now."

"Okay, so, you think this means we can stop talking about the Tenth Crusade, at least for tonight?" Malcolm asked. "Can I go get drunk and fall over now? I'd really like to fall over now."

Rami laughed. "You salty son of a bitch. But yes, lets end this nonsense. Plus, my friend Miranda will be here in an hour or so. I promise, you're gonna love her."

III.

"Well, you must be Miranda," Malcolm said as he reached out to shake hands with the ridiculously attractive redhead who'd just entered the bar. "Word on the street is that I'm going to love you."

"Oh, is that so?" Miranda asked and playfully chuckled. She shook Malcolm's hand and picked up a bottle of beer. Looking awkwardly around the room, she took a long sip from the cold, brown bottle.

"Well, that's what this weird, bastard, friend of mind said. Course, I'm pretty sure he's this insane CIA agent now hell bent on killing all Christians, so that makes his opinions debatable," Malcolm said jokingly. Miranda stared at him as her face grew grim. She pursed her lips together and began to turn away.

"Ahh, shit, look, I'm sorry," Malcolm said and lightly grabbed Miranda's arm, turning her back towards him. "You're Christian, aren't you?"

"There something wrong with that?" Miranda asked.

"No, no, I swear. I have nothing against Christians. I just have a really weird sense of humor. I promise. I'm far more into gorgeous women than I'm into bashing religion. Scouts honor."

Miranda laughed. "Yeah, I know I look about as

Romanus as you can get. I'm pale. I'm short. And I've got red hair halfway down my back. But my grandparents converted to Christianity way back in the Second Civil War and that's what I was raised with."

"That's amazing," Malcolm said smiling. "Really. That you know your ancestry that far back. That's awesome. Honestly, I was raised with a mix of both religions, neither religions, and a few Eastern religions. It made me a sort of in-between term called Agnostic. Ever heard of it?"

"A little," Miranda replied, opening up. "It means you're sort of on both sides, right? You believe in everything? Christianity and Romanus?"

"Kind of the opposite, really. It means I'm against both. I believe in neither. I'm open to both sides of the argument, but I take neither to heart. Believing in both sides would make me have to judge too many people. That's a lot of work. I'd rather judge no one. 'Make drinks, not war,' that's what I say. You're all okay, in my book," Malcolm said and chuckled.

"Awww, you're more Christian than you already know."

Malcolm sighed. "Man, if I had nickel for every time I heard that."

"What? Really?"

"No, actually. I'd be broke. No one's ever told me that before," Malcolm said, flashing his award-winning, shit-eating grin.

Miranda laughed and punched him in the arm. "Geez, you're an ass."

"Now that's more like it. If I had a nickel for every time I heard that. Hell. I'd be a billionaire. But doesn't being friends with Rami weird you out though? I mean, he isn't too fond of your kind."

"Yeah, I know. We just don't talk about it. Though I'm secretly trying to convert him. Shhhh." Miranda winked.

"Oooh, good luck on that one, sister. His family's

been Romanus for about fifty bajillion years. That what you do for a living then? Try to bring people to the dark side?"

Miranda laughed. "No, but it's a bit hard to explain. I work for a non-profit organization. We work with lawyers who defend criminals and help to put those individuals in treatment facilities, educational centers, or other places rather than prison. Sometimes we reduce their sentences, sometimes we get their charges dropped altogether."

Malcolm laughed. "So you keep criminals on the street then?"

"Hey, someone's gotta do it!"

"That doesn't worry you at all?"

"Not at all. It's simple, if you ask me. Someone needs to stand by these people. They've had no one to stand by them their whole lives. They've been told that since they're born, that they have eight major gods and three hundred other gods looking out for them but really, they just get left in the street. I like to think that if someone is standing by them, someone real and breathing, then they might actually fix themselves. I like to think that maybe I can be the one to make them feel responsible for their lives. Yeah, yeah, I know it sounds naïve and stupid. I know how Christian it sounds. I've heard it a hundred times. But you can't hate a girl for trying, right? For fighting for people who've never had anyone fight for them in their lives? That has to mean something, doesn't it?"

"Wow," Malcolm said, stunned. "Holy crap, that was hot. That might be the most powerful argument for being a Christian I've ever heard. It's too bad I only have that one nickel I earned from you earlier. Cause right now I really wanna buy you a drink and I don't think five cents is gonna cut the mustard."

"You're not kidding," Miranda said and smiled. "If you had a couple more, I'd probably let you buy me dinner."

"Aw, crap, really? Damn my one nickel!" Malcolm said and feigned disappointment. "Guess you'll just have to settle and let me cook dinner for you instead."

"Oh?" Miranda asked and very overdramatically rested her head on her hands. "Go on."

"How do you feel about braised duck legs with a hearts of palm salad on the side?"

"Shut up!" Miranda said as she pulled herself back and grabbed Malcolm's arm. "Duck and palm trees? Oh my god, that might be my most favorite meal ever!"

Malcolm burst out laughing. "Did you just call hearts of palm, 'palm trees'?"

"Well that's what they are, aren't they?" she asked and smirked innocently enough.

"Ah, hell," Malcolm said as he nodded his head. "Rami was right."

"Right about what?"

"I am gonna love you, aren't I?"

IV.

"You're a fucking asshole," Malcolm yelled out as he took a sip of bourbon. He wasn't even looking at Rami, who had just entered the bar. It was early afternoon on a Saturday and so the bar was mostly empty. No one even glanced up from their conversations as Malcolm screamed obscenities across the room.

"Yeah, it's good to see you, too," Rami said as he walked over and sat down on the stool next to Malcolm. He loosened his tie and hailed down the bartender. "A vodka and soda, please," he said. Malcolm looked over at him with outright disgust.

"Yeah, yeah, whatever, dick," Rami said. "I know, it's a pussy drink. Have all the laughs you want. Bottom line is, I weigh thirty more pounds than you do. When we get into a five percent weight ratio, I'll start pounding the bourbon again. Deal?"

Malcolm nodded his head and raised his eyebrows. "Fair enough."

"Thank you."

"So, how goes the ol' espionage business this week? Overthrow any nations over lunch?"

"Here's the thing...." Rami began.

"Oh fuck, I just walked into a bee's nest didn't I?"

"We used Christians as slaves for nigh on two thousand something years. Their original homeland is completely dominated by the Muslims that laid claim to the land well over a millennium ago. And we only even granted them their freedom a hundred and fifty years ago. They, as a people, are a bit on edge. I get that part. I really do. Especially since the piece of land they're asking for is already populated 85% by Christians and lies right on the border of our country and Mexico.

"My problem is not with any of that though. My problem is that their viewpoints on society are radically and violently different from ours and people don't realize that. On top of that, on a personal level, they are near opposites from everything my family believes in. We're House of Ares, Mal. The House of War. You know they believe in total peace, right? Killing is a sin? Malcolm, for me and my family, killing is a virtue. Giving a serious voice to the Christians means giving a serious voice to the people who would see my religious beliefs be destroyed. I mean, one God? One?! Have you ever heard of such a stupid thing?"

"But..."

"On top of that, the Eight Major Houses can't agree on shit right now. They've been deadlocked on this issue for nearly a decade. They've just all ganged up together on two sides and neither will budge. Which is completely fucking absurd cause our entire political structure was based on *multiple* ideas being brought to an arena for discussion – eight to be exact – and then a plan that suits everyone agreed upon. But this one thing or the other crap? It's retarded. Nothing will ever get done ever again if it keeps up."

"Wow, Rami," Malcolm began. "All I asked is how your day had been. How hard would it have been to say,

'I'm in the middle of an impossible civil war against a small population that is gaining a popular foothold and could undermine our entire political structure?'"

"Shut it. I'll have you assassinated so fast it'll make your head spin."

"Ah, maybe tomorrow," Malcolm said. He shrugged his shoulders and took a sip of his bourbon

"Thank Gods," Rami said as he hailed down the bartender and ordered another vodka and soda. "Assassinations are so much fucking paperwork." Rami took a sip of his drink and casually looked over at Malcolm. "So what's good in the editing world, kid? Your life must be so much less interesting than mine."

Malcolm burst out laughing. "Two shots," Malcolm said as the bartender delivered Rami's drink. "Tequila."

"Uh oh, what'd you do wrong now, you fucking idiot?"

"You know your friend Miranda? The court advocate? The Christian girl who loves everyone and wants to save everyone? That stupid fucking bitch who thinks peace beyond all eight fucking Gods and her Jesus guy is possible and wants to create a fucking utopia among this stupid goddamn planet of ours?"

"You're in love with her, aren't you?"

"Of course I am! Shit, why do you think I'm so pissed off at you?"

Rami chuckled and took back his shot of tequila. Malcolm did the same. "So what's the big problem then?" Rami asked.

"Well, first of all, I'm in love with her. That's a big enough problem in itself. You know how batshit insane I am. I called my mother yesterday, for no reason at all! Just to say hi! Me! I did that! This is what she's doing to me. You really think this is healthy for me?"

"Okay, okay, that's hard to argue," Rami said as he laughed. "But we both know that's not the big issue here. What's really going on?"

Malcolm looked down at the bar as he absentmindedly spun his drink around with his right hand. He ground his teeth and tapped his feet to the song that was playing on the jukebox. All the while, it was disgustingly obvious how uncomfortable he was with Rami's question.

Eventually, Malcolm took a deep breath and blurted out a few words. "So, it's like this," he said.

"Karly Nosmith is in love with you, isn't she?" Rami asked calmly as he sipped on his drink.

"Karly Nosmith is in lo…" Malcolm said at the exact same time, but stopped as Rami repeated the sentence he was about to say, word for word. "How the hell do you do that?"

Rami laughed. "Told you it was bound to happen sooner or later, sucker." He took a big sip of his drink and ordered a third round from the waitress. Malcolm just stared at him with shock and awe. "Ah, come off it, you bastard. You know I know everything. Are you positive though? This isn't just all in your head?"

"Well, we haven't talked about it per say, but Karly's definitely been acting weird. She's been asking me what I'm doing and who I'm hanging out with all the time lately. And we'll be naked in bed doing the post-sex cuddle and, I swear, she practically breaks down in tears when I have to get up to take a piss. It's just a hundred little things like that. She's definitely got it in her head that we aren't just friends with benefits anymore and she's slowly but surely getting tired of pretending that's the case."

"Alright, well, the real question is, what are you gonna do about it?"

"How do you mean?"

"Well, you're in love with Miranda. Is she in love with you?"

"I think so."

"You think so?"

"Well, the other day, we woke up in bed together and she looked at me and said, 'Malcolm, I think I'm in love with you.' That work for you?"

"Exactly how big is your dick?" Rami asked. "Got

all these gorgeous women falling in love with you left and right. Fucking hell. And you're talking like you want me to feel bad for you. Piss off."

Malcolm laughed. "Well, word on the street is that I am an asshole. Maybe try that?"

"Hell, it's as good advice as any, you sack of dicks. And it's only been what? Three months since you met, Miranda? Geez, you do fast work. But anyway, what about Karly?"

Malcolm took a deep breath and let it out in a long, exasperated sigh.

"What about Karly?" Rami repeated.

"I love Karly. To death. But I don't want to date her. I don't want to marry her. I don't want to end up with her. I don't want to....I don't know, finish the sentence for yourself."

"Well, you need to tell her that. Right now. Before it gets worse."

"Really? That's your great insight? Aren't you the one who told me to be wary of the wrath of the Oracle? What she might to do me if I ever hurt her? This is your great advice? Just tell her?"

"Can we get two more shots of tequila?" Rami asked as the bartender came past them again. "Okay, well, you're about to experience that wrath regardless. So, either own up to it now or drag it out and wait till it gets even worse. The choice is up to you, brother. But you said it yourself: Karly's a Christian now. So, just confess your sins and let her forgiveness wash over you. You either believe it or you don't. But stop being a baby and put some big boy pants on already."

"I hate it when you're right," Malcolm said.

"So you just hate me all the time then, huh?"

"Jackwagon."

Rami took a long, slow breath. He looked over at Malcolm and calculated a lot of outcomes and realities out in his head. Then he placed a hand on Malcolm's back, finished his drink, and spoke. "Look, with any luck, you'll have the rest of your life to think about this question. When it was asked of me, I only had about ten minutes. So, please, consider it sincerely and deeply: Why was Louis XVI the greatest king France ever had?"

"Huh? Is that a trick question? Wasn't he the king that caused the French Revolution? Wasn't he the worst king? You're asking me how he was actually the greatest?"

"I am. Just give it a good thought, will you? Why was Louis XVI France's greatest king? Think about it really, really hard."

"Okay, great, will do, you drunken idiot. I'll think long and hard about that. And the amazing advice you gave me about Karly."

"Try to remember," Rami began, "I'm always right. Your life will only get easier and easier as you come to accept that."

V.

Karly held Malcolm's hand and rubbed his thumb and forefinger slowly. The two had their hands intertwined underneath Karly's favorite table at a local seafood restaurant she had been frequenting for years. The owners knew her and always kept a back corner table reserved for her, should she want to come in. Of course, that didn't really matter since hardly anyone ever recognized the Oracle in public. Seeing a demi-goddess in jeans and a t-shirt with her hair in a ponytail usually threw most people off their game.

For Malcolm though, it was old news. And while they were waiting for their entrees to be served, it was right around then that Karly had started to get frisky and sentimental. Malcolm was not exactly into it; hell, Malcolm was pretty over it. He had been thinking for days about how best to tell Karly what was really going on. In the end, he came up with precisely nothing. His best idea had been to take her to her favorite restaurant and plea for mercy.

Thirty minutes into the meal and Malcolm was realizing exactly how stupid of a plan that was. He spent most of that time calling Rami a colorful assortment of insults in his head. All this while Karly caressed his hand and licked her lips in a way that made his blood flow into places he prefer it didn't.

It was right about then that a very weird feeling washed over Malcolm. Here he was, exactly no one to no one, and promptly ready to reject the Oracle of Babylon once and for all. This was either the bravest thing he'd ever done or the outright dumbest.

Malcolm was pretty sure it was the latter.

"Hey, Karly," he began. "We've known each other for a long ass time now, yeah? Ten years is it?"

"Just a little over ten years," she replied. "It was ten years last month."

Malcolm laughed. "Wow, I can't believe you remember it to that detail. That's when we met in that old dive bar where my friend's band was playing, huh? Freaking crazy. Who knew this would've gone on that long?"

"Right?!" Karly asked, also incredulous. "I mean, isn't that just ridiculous? Ten years since we've been having this affair. You'd almost think there was something more behind it." That's when she shot Malcolm a set of bedroom eyes that made him want to simultaneously jump her in the middle of the restaurant and violently shit his own pants.

Malcolm deflected. "Yeah, but how many guys have you fallen in love with since we've met? At least five, right?"

Karly briefly wriggled in her seat and thought. "Sounds about right. I mean, I guess I was married twice. They have to count for something. Though, let's be honest. I did cheat on both of them with you, Malcolm," she said and smiled deviously.

That was roughly when Malcolm prayed Jupiter,

Jesus, Krishna, or even fucking Mohammed would just strike him down with a lightning bolt and kill him already.

"Look, Karly, I'm sorry, but I can't do this anymore," Malcolm finally blurted out. Karly pulled her hand away and glared at him. That's when the waiter approached with impeccable timing and put their two entrees down on the table. Not needing to be a fucking psychic, the waiter promptly realized that the tension level at the table was severe enough to do a tightrope routine on. He only nodded his head and walked away. Malcolm just stared at his plate of coconut crusted shrimp, lacking the strength to look Karly in the eye.

"Can't do what anymore?" she asked in a tone that Malcolm had never heard before. It was a pretty unpleasant tone. He could've gone on with the rest of his life pretty happily without ever having heard it.

Malcolm gritted his teeth and let his leg shake involuntarily. "There's this girl I met a few months ago. She...she's pretty great. And, well, I've got some feelings for her. A lot of them, really."

"A....a girl?" Karly whispered and withdrew herself from Malcolm.

"I know this is weird, Karly. Really. But, she's even a Christian. You'd love her, really. I mean..."

"Are you breaking up with me?" Karly asked, eyes wide.

"Well, were we ever really together?" Malcolm hated himself before he even finished asking the question. His eyes went wide with surprised disgust like someone else was saying it. Even halfway through it, when he knew he should stop speaking, he couldn't. And while he sat there, amazed with himself, Karly looked at him like he had punched her in the back of the head and then ejaculated in her face.

Well, in the way she didn't like, that is.

"Look, Karly, I didn't mean that," he said and reached his hands out to her. Karly withdrew herself back into the booth.

"Please, just, don't," she said as she looked away from him. "Malcolm, you know…you know we have a lot…."

"We have a lot of history? A lot of romance? A love of great times? Hell, Karly, even a lot of sincere love and affection for each other. Yes, I agree to all that. But you've had your hand with a lot of other guys. Can't you let me have my hand with just one other girl? Even a girl of your own faith? She's a Christian, Karly. Can't you forgive me?"

Karly stood up from the dinner table. "Yes, Malcolm, I can forgive you."

"Then…."

"But it doesn't mean we all forgive you. And it doesn't mean I have to like it."

"What does that mean?" Malcolm asked, confused.

"Just that you should be careful, Malcolm. Not everyone is a kind, forgiving Christian like I am."

With that, Karly walked out of the restaurant and hailed a taxi. Malcolm didn't quite understand what had happened, but he hoped and prayed that this was the end of the ordeal. He wasn't happy that Karly clearly hated him for the moment, but he figured time would heal her wounds. He quickly ate, paid the check, and went home hoping the worst of his troubles were over.

VI.

Malcolm stood at Rami's front door and pounded on it hard enough to set off a nearby car alarm. In between beatings, he rang the front door bell dozens of times and shouted at the top of his lungs. Twice a car drove by and he ran after it, down in the middle of the road, screaming of social injustice. This went on for about twenty minutes on a random, Thursday evening at two in the morning.

"You have ten seconds to convince me why I

shouldn't call the cops," Rami said through bloodshot eyes as he finally came downstairs to see what his friend was having a coronary over.

Malcolm quickly walked up to Rami and, without even flinching, punched him in the face as hard as he could. As Rami began to recover, Malcolm punched him again, laying his friend down on the pavement. That's when Malcolm climbed on top of Rami and wound up again. Rami only saved himself from a further beating by grabbing Malcolm's arm in mid-air.

"Anything you'd like to talk about, Mal?" Rami asked, almost casually.

"Where the fuck is she?!" was all Malcolm could say. He continued to try and force himself down on Rami.

"As fun as this is, I'd prefer to continue this conversation in my living room over some bourbon. Do you agree?"

"No, you psychotic CIA fuck! What did you do with Miranda?" Malcolm tried to hit Rami again but failed miserably.

"Ah, well, now we're getting somewhere," Rami said, still holding back Malcolm's arms. "Of course, the good question is what makes you think I have something to do with her disappearance."

"Karly said that..." Malcolm began.

"Ahhh, Karly said," Rami interrupted. "Interesting notion." At that, Malcolm relaxed a bit. "Come on, old boy. Come inside and have a drink. Let's talk about your missing girl."

Malcolm climbed off Rami and dusted himself off. Then he followed Rami inside his home and, as he had done a hundred times before, poured himself a glass of bourbon and sat down on his couch. He took a sip and tried to relax. Rami came out of the kitchen with an ice pack on the side of his face.

"If this swells up, my bosses are gonna be pissed. Luckily, you hit like a ninety-year old woman. So, what exactly is going on now? And what did Karly say?"

"She said that not everyone is a kind, forgiving Christian like she is. It just sort of seemed cryptic and bitchy at the time, which I can't say I blamed her for. But now Miranda's gone missing. I haven't heard from her in two days and she hadn't been to work. That's when I went to her apartment and found the place torn to shit. I called her sister and she didn't know anything either. So I started thinking about what Karly said and about how not everyone is a kind, forgiving Christian. That made me think about who I know who hated Christians. Who'd want to see them behind bars. And I hate to be a dick, Rami, but that's you."

Rami chuckled. "Okay, that's not all true, but I see your point. Though there's a bigger question you've been too blind with anger to think about: What motivation do I have to make Miranda disappear?"

"That's obvious," Malcolm began. "You only recently found out she was a Christian when I talked to you about her. And you're worried she's going to poison the mind of your best friend. Not to mention that her career involves putting criminals back on the street which I imagine your bosses aren't too happy about. They're all small reasons in and of themselves, but combined, it's pretty clear as to why you'd want her out of the picture.

"So I'm gonna ask again. This time more nicely. Where the fuck is my girlfriend?"

Rami sighed. Long and hard. "Really, Malcolm? That's what you think?"

"Yes, it is. You have a better idea?"

"Malcolm, you realize it was me who introduced you to Miranda, right?"

"Yeah, so, you might not have known about her..."

"I've known about everything she's done since she was three years old. None of us care about it even to the smallest degree. She pays her taxes. She isn't rallying anyone. And you're not exactly a shining example of Romanus citizenry to begin with. The amount of money it takes to kidnap someone in the middle of the night and bring them to a secret facility is not well spent on the likes of Miranda Stauffer."

"So then what then? Where is she? What's happened to her? Who would do this?"

"I think you need to think a little harder, Mal. There's only one person who hates Miranda enough to make her disappear."

"Wait, Karly? You think Karly did this?" Malcolm asked incredulously. "How? She's the Oracle of Babylon. I mean, she's a Christian, not some sort of secret..."

"If the shoe fits?" Rami asked and shrugged his shoulders.

"What?! How does the shoe fit? That makes no fucking sense?!"

"It doesn't?"

"No! It's totally...totally...wait...no...NO!"

"Sorry to be the bearer of bad news, kid, but...."

"No!" Malcolm yelled out again. "She can't...She can't be!"

VII.

Malcolm stormed through the Cave of the Oracle like a full-strength hurricane birthed out of the ninth circle of Hell. He knocked down every candle he passed; he defaced every rune he approached; he spoke every offense and screamed out every profanity he could think of.

"Karly Evelyn Nosmith!" Malcolm bellowed out. He was standing in the Oracle's ante-chamber. "What have you done with her?!"

Karly Nosmith, the Oracle of Babylon, one of the most powerful women in the Western World, walked out of her back room wearing what she called her War Suit. Malcolm couldn't help but freeze. There were few things on the planet that could compare to the Oracle's War Suit.

This was because when the Oracle went to war, she intended to win.

The Oracle's War Suit was simple. It was stark nudity. Karly walked out toward Malcolm in full make up, in full hair, in high heels, and in immaculate, naked perfection.

"You really want to ruin all this?" she said casually to Malcolm's gaping mouth and bloodshot eyes.

For three seconds, he forgot about Miranda Stauffer. Looking at the Oracle in her War Suit, it wasn't exactly unreasonable. Hell, it would've been unreasonable if he *hadn't* forgot about Miranda. But still, only three seconds was pretty commendable. Under certain conditions, he'd probably be given a Purple Heart and made a Three Star General. You win a war like that and you should be given every fucking accolade the universe has to offer you.

"I don't want to ruin all that," Malcolm said as he turned away. "I just want to know where my girlfriend is."

"And what makes you think I had something to do with it?"

"You were never really a Christian, were you?" he asked.

"Oh, come on, sweetie. I'm the Oracle of Babylon. You really thought I had become a Christian? Don't be silly now," Karly spoke condescendingly as she continued to approach Malcolm, one deceptive step at a time.

"So what? You're some sort of double agent? You pretend to be a Romanus to most; the great Oracle of Babylon. Of course, anyone who gets close to you or who's thinking of rebelling will soon find out you're a Christian. Or, pretending to be, at least. They'll confide in you. And soon, they'll all be arrested. You pretend to be a Christian to get their trust. And then you use that trust against them.

"Except in my case, you just fucked me over cause you're a jealous, fucking bitch. Miranda wasn't some sort of Christian tactical rebel and you know it; she was just my girlfriend. A simple girl who's favorite fucking food was sandwiches of all things. You've had dozens and dozens of men worship you throughout your life. But gods fucking forbid I have one girl that actually liked me! Why, Karly? Why did you decide to just royally fuck me over? What did I ever do to you? *What?*"

"You said no to me," Karly said simply and began to cry. "No one had ever said no to me, Malcolm. No one. Much less you. *You!* It was....Malcolm, how am I supposed to take no for an answer from my best lover and my best friend? *How?*" She finally was within arm's reach of Malcolm and softly brushed his chin with her manicured fingernails. He hated himself for enjoying the sensation and the goosebumps which ran down his back.

Malcolm deflated. "Please, Karly, don't make this harder than it already is on me. You know I'm not doing this out of spite. Out of anger. I love you. I really do. But I love you as a person and not as a wife. You know taking Miranda from me isn't right. I know you do. Somewhere in that crazy, mixed-up head of yours, you know what you did is wrong. I mean, how would you feel if someone took me from you? How angry would you be? How upset? How miserable? Please don't do that back to me, just out of spite. You know I'd never do that to you. You know I'd never even want to see you that sad."

The Oracle of Babylon looked up at Malcolm. That's when he saw endless streams of saltwater etch cheerless canals across her high cheekbones. "You're right. You wouldn't. Oh, Gods, you win," she whispered, her voice hardly more than a raspy whisper.

"That's it?" Malcolm asked, surprised she would cave so easily.

Karly sniffled. "You'd never fight like this for me. Which means you don't care about me enough. You care about her more. You'd destroy the cave of an Oracle to get her back. I can't compete with that."

"Karly, I…"

"No, please, Malcolm. You win. You did what no man has ever done. You've broken the Oracle of Babylon's heart. If that isn't a feat worthy of a reward, then I don't know what is."

VIII.

"Are you sure those were exact words?" Rami asked.

"Yeah, why?" Malcolm replied.

"That's not good."

"How so?"

"Look, Mal, I hate to say this, but Karly is not the young stripper you once came to know and love. She's deceitful and psychotic. She's forgotten what it's like to not be worshipped as a demi-goddess. Luckily for you, I know a thing or two about deceitful and psychotic."

"Okay, so, you don't think she's gonna let her go then? What do you think she's gonna do?"

"I think she's going to kill her. And I think she might even do it herself."

"Ah," Malcolm said calmly.

"That's it? 'Ah'?"

"Ah, Malcolm continued. "So this is what a nervous breakdown feels like." Malcolm promptly then slid off Rami's couch and onto the floor knocking over a side table in the process. Whisky and pasta soared through the air before coming to a crash all across Rami's living room. Rami didn't even get up. Didn't even flinch. He just watched as his carpets and couch cushions got doused in tomato sauce and bourbon. After a few seconds, Rami sucked on his teeth and turned back to Malcolm.

"I'm sending you a bill for that, just so you know. Fucking overdramatic actress," he said indifferently.

"You think you can do anything to help her?" Malcolm asked, totally ignoring Rami's threat of a hefty dry cleaning bill. "Please, I'll do anything. This is my fault. I have to do something to make it right."

"Oh, calm down already. Of course there's something I can do to help her. The problem is that she's more than likely already been charged with something pretty heinous. I mean, Karly can't just go to the Department of Foresight and say 'this girl's a threat' and they go and pick her up. She must've falsified some evidence to get Miranda detained. And I don't know how long that will take me to legally undo. And I don't know if Miranda will live long enough to see that happen."

"Well, you're just a ray of sunshine, aren't you?"

"Look, let me make some phone calls and check up on some things. I have some favors owed to me. But, if I do manage to sneak her out of wherever she is, she'll still end up being an enemy of the state. Best case scenario, you'll have ten minutes with her before we put her on a plane to Guatemala or some such shit."

Malcolm looked at the floor to his right and saw that there was still a little bit of whisky left in his upturned glass. He picked it up and emptied the few remaining drops into his mouth. "Do it. I'll go with her wherever she goes. It's the very least I owe her."

Rami sighed and looked at his broken friend. "Well, let's hope she feels the same way," he whispered under his breath.

IX.

Malcolm stood on the tarmac at Westchester Airport with a suitcase in one hand and a bouquet of flowers in the other. It was three in the morning and the cloud-filled sky blocked even the brightest star from being visible. Malcolm hadn't called his family. He hadn't called any other friends. No one knew he was leaving. He was too scared at this point that he might screw something else up and lose Miranda forever. He'd rather disappear into the sunset with her than risk losing her.

Eventually, a black van with dark tinted windows pulled up onto the tarmac and stopped a few dozen feet in front of him. The passenger door opened and Rami stepped outside. Malcolm's eyes widened as he saw his friend dressed in a full, ceremonial military suit. Numerous medals and bars of rank and other such ornaments adorned the left breast of his dark green jacket. Rami looked straight at Malcolm and swallowed hard. Malcolm couldn't quite place the expression on his friend's face, but before he had time to figure it out, Rami turned and slid open the van door.

Her wrists bound in handcuffs, Miranda stepped out into the bright halogen lights of the tarmac. Immediately, Malcolm could see bruises and gashes all over her face and neck. Reflexively, he threw the flowers down on the ground and ran as fast as he could over to her. He practically tackled her as he wrapped his arms around her and kissed her neck. "Oh gods, what did they do to you?" he repeated over and over as his sinuses began to shut down and his tear ducts began to bulge.

Two other men, also dressed in military suits, climbed out of the van behind Miranda and looked around cautiously. They spoke into hidden microphones and listened on earpieces as a small propeller airplane began to approach the five of them.

"Malcolm," Miranda said, her voice like rocks in a muddy riverbed, "I need to ask you something."

"Of course," he said and pulled away from Miranda to look into her eyes. "Anything."

"When I asked you if you were seeing anyone else and you said 'no', did you really mean to say, 'I'm fucking the Oracle of Babylon, a psychotic bitch I've known for ten years and who is also in love with me?'"

Malcolm promptly became exsanguinated. He lost all sensation in his outer extremities and saw the entire world before him go cloudy and blurry. The only thing that was real for him – the only solid thing in all the universe – was Miranda's physically beaten face which glared back at him not with hate, not with anguish, but with simple indifference.

"I...I...I never..."

"Perfect," she said as she turned her head toward Rami. "All I needed to hear. Let's go." The two other men in the van then each lightly held one of Miranda's arms and began to walk her to the airplane. She struggled to keep pace with them and after only a few steps, buckled and nearly collapsed onto the black asphalt. The only thing that kept her up were the two men's steady hands.

"No, please, I'm sorry," Malcolm pleaded. "Oh, holy fuck, if there's ever been anything I've ever been sorry about in my entire life, it's this. I had no idea what Karly was capable of. And I...god, I can't believe I didn't end it with her sooner. Or that I never told you. God, Miranda, you were just too amazing. I was falling for you faster than I knew what to do with and I made a lot of mistakes. Mistakes that I will hate myself for till the day I die. Please, please, don't let it end like this. Please, at least let me go with you and make sure you're healed and taken care of. Then you can kick me out if you want. But, please, don't let it end like this. Please forgive me and give me another chance."

Miranda hesitated. Then, with the help of her escorts, she slowly turned around. "Of course I forgive you, Malcolm. You made an honest mistake. And if I was your advocate in court, I'd be completely behind you.

"But forgiveness and trust are two different things. It's really hard for me to trust you right now, Mal. Even you must see that. Maybe that'll change one day. I sure hope it will." And with that, she hobbled back around and finished making her way into the plane.

"How?" Malcolm begged. "How do I regain your trust if I don't even know where you're going?"

"That's what you have him for," Miranda said and looked over at Rami. "You really think I'm ever gonna go anywhere for the rest of my life that he doesn't know about?" Then she smiled, big and bright despite all her pain and confusion. "I'll see you around, Mal."

Before Malcolm even knew what else to say, the

door was closed and the plane was slowly making its way down the runway. Malcolm stood there, stunned, and watched as the first girl he'd loved in his adult life slowly sped off and flew away into the night sky. Eventually, Rami came up behind him and put an arm around his shoulders. "Come on, man. I think I owe you a beer, at the very least."

X.

Dear Miranda,

It always feels weird writing these letters. I just put a few pieces of paper into an envelope and hand them to Rami and assume they're going to you and not into the desk of some clerk who couldn't care less about you and I. Hell, I don't even know if you couldn't care less about you and I. You've never written me back. Or maybe you have and the CIA's letter delivery service just isn't up to snuff. Either way, I like to imagine you're getting these letters. I hope you get at least some comfort from them, wherever you are, despite all the reckless harm I caused in your life.

Anyway, sorry. I'm rambling again. Like always. I actually just have a couple quick things to say in this letter and then I'll be done. Maybe forever. This may or may not be the last letter you actually ever get from me. Because, basically, I've decided to leave the country. This whole place has just gotten too insane. I mean, a girl I'd known for a significant portion of my life was lying to my face about being a secret agent. Not to mention that Rami is also a secret agent. And get this, he's actually more of a secret agent than I even thought he was.

I spent a long time wondering why he would bother risking his life to save you. I know that sounds harsh, but it's true. I know he's my friend and he's your friend and those are good enough reasons on their own, but in saving you, he defied the Oracle. And his bosses. And he got two other people to go along with him. He was more or less risking his own execution and the execution of two others just to get you out of jail. That's exceptionally bold.

Not long after that, Rami sort of went off the deep end. We started hanging less and less cause his anti-Christian stances and CIA politics were getting a little ridiculous. You know how I tried to stay out of all that nonsense like you did, but it got to the point where it was impossible. I could hardly stand to be around him.

Which became more and more confusing as to why he'd save your life even though he knew you were a Christian. Again, yeah, your friend, my girlfriend, I know. But something just didn't add up.

That's when I started thinking about this really weird question he asked me way back when I told him about you and Karly. 'Why was Louis XVI France's greatest king?' I thought he was nuts for a long time since Louis XVI was the guy that caused the French Revolution. He was the bastard of all bastards. What could he possibly have done that was great?

The answer is insane. You may or not even believe it since I'm not even sure I do. But the great thing Louis did was actually cause the French Revolution. Before him, it was kings and tyrants. After him, it was democracy. We all consider him this great oppressor but what if he was the opposite? What if he wanted his people to be free and knew that the only way they'd stand up for themselves was to choke them? That in choking them, they'd hit back. What if he pretended to be a tyrant just to free his people?

What if Rasputin did the same with Russia? What if King George III did the same with America? What if Constantine, nearly two thousand years ago, tried to do the same with the Christians and failed miserably? What if all these tyrants were really saviors?

That's when I realized what Rami was. Another double agent. A Christian who's been posing as an anti-Christian for god knows how many years just to weasel his way into the government and apply pressure where it's needed. He's another savior posing as a tyrant. And apparently there's a whole network of them. But, so of course, this would mean he'd hardly be able to stand one of his Christian friends actually being oppressed and tortured. He'd have to save you. After all, it's all he wants.

That was more or less the last straw for me. After that, I realized there was no one in this country left that I could trust. And I knew how you must've felt when you found out about me. I suddenly stopped caring about the US. About the Tenth Crusade. About the Christian nation. All I wanted was to be somewhere safe. Somewhere sound. And so, I packed my bags, hugged my friends goodbye, and by the time you read this, I should be resettled in Auckland, New Zealand. I've got an old friend there who owns a bar and he said I could bartend until I got my shit together. Which means I'll be working there for at least a decade. Ha.

Oh, and one last thing. When I told Rami about my whole problem with you and Karly, you know what his advice was? Tell Karly flat out. Now, honestly, I keep thinking about it, and that's some pretty shitty advice. You know what I think was really going on? I think Rami knew how shitty it was. I think he was trying to do the same thing with you and me as he's doing with the Christians. I think he was trying to destroy us a little bit to make us a lot better. I think he knew we needed a revolution and that's the only way it was going to happen.

In some ways, he was right. But, unfortunately for him, I think he over did it. Before the victim was able to fight back and overtake the oppressor, the victim died. We didn't make it. But I don't blame him. He tried his best. You tried your best. I'm the only one who could've tried a lot harder. And now, I don't know what else to try other than leaving this weird, deranged country and seeking my fortune elsewhere.

Goodbye, gorgeous. I'll never stop thinking about you. And I'll always be a better person for you destroying that small part of me.

Forever yours,
Malcolm

XI.

Two months later, Malcolm picked up an empty beer bottle off the bar and threw it out. One of his afternoon regulars stumbled out of the bar and into the street. Malcolm wiped down the dirty parts of the bar where the elderly man had been sitting and then turned to wash some dirty glasses.

Suddenly, the door swung open and a petite girl walked in and stood in the middle of the bar. Malcolm noticed her out of the corner of his eye, but didn't pay her any special attention.

"Happy hour till seven, darlin'. What'll it be?" Malcolm said as he turned the sink off and dried off his waterlogged hands off on an old towel. Still the girl said nothing. She just took slow, silent steps forward and moved some hair out of her face, waiting for Malcolm to really notice her.

"What, you can't…" Malcolm began to say, but stopped speaking the moment he looked up. His spine immediately turned to ice and his lungs collapsed into iron knots. He was no longer a human, just a beautifully sculpted piece of flesh neither capable of movement nor thought.

The two stared at each other for a long, long time before finally, at long last, one of them said something.

"Hi," Miranda Stauffer said and smiled. "Word on the street is that I'm going to love you."

ABOUT THE AUTHOR

J.E. Tobal was born and raised in south Florida. Many people would argue that this has ruined him for life. He left as soon as he was able and moved to New York City. It's a smidge colder there, but there's also a lot less alligators and deadly snakes around. He's fine with this.

Since graduating from New York University with a degree in English, he has written everything from novels to short stories to comic books to short films. He continues to reside in New York City with neither wife, nor child, nor canine companion.

Chances are, he doesn't like you.

Made in the USA
Lexington, KY
11 November 2019